W9-CKL-085

THE PERFECT PLACE

THE
PERFECT

ALFRED A. KNOPF NEW YORK 1989

PLACE

a novel by

Sheila Kohler

THIS IS A BORZOI BOOK
PUBLISHED BY ALFRED A. KNOPF, INC.

Published in the United States by Alfred A. Knopf, Inc.,
New York, and simultaneously in Canada by Random
House of Canada Limited, Toronto. Distributed
by Random House, Inc., New York.

A portion of this book was originally published in
The Quarterly and was thereafter selected for reprint
in *Prize Stories: The O. Henry Awards*, 1988.

Library of Congress Cataloging-in-Publication Data
Kohler, Sheila.
The perfect place.
I. Title
PR9369.3.K64T4 1989 823 88-45490
ISBN 0-394-57373-0

Manufactured in the United States of America

FIRST EDITION

For Maxine (1939–1979),
and with gratitude to
Gordon Lish, my teacher

THE MOUNTAIN

The man I met in Gerzett—I believe I met him in Gerzett; I cannot be certain—said something about a fly. It was what he said about the fly that made me remember.

At any rate, I did not notice the man coming toward me because I was reading or sipping a cup of tea or doing both, or perhaps I was simply gazing at the lake. I was looking across the smooth green grass that dipped down toward the lake like a sigh and saw, I think, the silver blue of the water reflected for a moment in the breast of a bird as it swept across my vision.

Naturally, I did not notice the man.

He was not really the sort one notices, even coming toward one, even in those shoes: thick crepe-soled shoes that give beneath the foot with a slight lurch and squeak mournfully as one moves. Besides, I was accustomed to handling this sort of thing, or what I thought was this sort of thing. I went on doing whatever it was I had been doing before.

Even when the fellow was quite close to me, getting in the way of my afternoon light, his shadow before him, I did not look up. It usually works best—ignoring them—I mean, if that is what they are after, which this fellow in fact was not. When he began to speak, I did not even hear what he was saying to me until he had said it twice, and even then it was only the name that I heard. It was the name that struck me; it was not the sort of name one would forget entirely.

All of that month of May I had lingered on somewhat reluctantly in Gerzett. Despite what the physicians had told me about the therapeutic quality of the Swiss air, I found that the place was far too altitudinal for me; the rarefied air kept me constantly breathless.

I definitely did not appreciate the lake. Just the thought of that still, trapped water was somehow dreadfully depressing. But it was the mountains, those towering snow-tipped peaks, with their steep craggy treeless surfaces that filled me with an almost physical malaise, an impression of being shut in, or perhaps it was shut out.

Actually, I've never been able to remain for any extended period in the mountains. There is something about their stark beauty brooding eternally above one that daunts me and gives me a sense of the impoverishment of life, an impression of doom that can literally bring on an attack of nausea or breathlessness in my particular constitution.

To tell you the truth, I have never been particularly partial to Switzerland. The people are courteous, of course, but frightfully dull, and the whole place has always looked somehow "preserved" to me, rather like pickles in a jar. And too many cows, I always say, there are just far too many cows, and as for those wretched cowbells that wake one in the morning and ring constantly through the day, they are enough to send one rushing off into that lake.

The hotel, which had been recommended to me as secluded and well appointed, turned out, of course, to be somewhat dilapidated. It was quiet, naturally, surrounded as it was by acres of lawns and wooded areas and that depressing lake. There were the usual sort of mixed borders and spreading oaks and sad cypresses. But the whole place was not a little in need of repair. It had seen better days.

Actually, it rather amazed me that the place had any clients at all. It was one of those hotels so refined in its elegance that the elegance was really perceptible only in the price of the room. The bathrooms, though fortunately very clean, had undoubtedly not been altered for years, and the walls of the corridors and dining rooms had been painted a ghastly pale lime green that seemed to glow with an almost spectral light.

At that time of year, there was hardly anyone there except a handful of solid English dowagers whom I heard at mealtimes rather than saw, bent over their plates, beside the potted palms, scraping their way noisily through the indigestible food in the vast half-empty dining room.

However, I must say, I had managed to secure a not

entirely uncomfortable room after a long and vituperative argument with the hotel manager. I insisted on that particular accommodation because it was at some distance from the main body of the hotel, almost entirely self-contained and consequently very quiet—I suffer from insomnia and almost anything wakes me—and because of the honeysuckle that climbed up the wall and almost into my window.

The gardener had been obliged to cut back the honeysuckle from the window while I was staying in that room. He had hacked at the plants with a blunt instrument, a short semicircular blade or sickle, and I had told him not to prune the creeper too drastically but to let it climb along the windowsill so that I could admire it from my bed when I woke in the mornings.

The room was large and sunny with a wide, soft double bed and a reading lamp that you could actually read by, a rarity in hotels, I always find; and a steel table and chair on a not unbearably narrow, private area where I was able to enjoy the weather that was, I will admit, passably fair for that time of year, I imagine: the light clear and bright from dawn to sunset and the wind still.

And the physicians, after all, had gone on at considerable length to recommend the place to me, praising the dry, pure air and the sunny climate, what they had the audacity to call the plain healthy food, and pointing out that the secluded nature and general restfulness of the place was ideal for someone suffering from my eternal complaint; so I lingered on for a while, partly out of apathy—the spring has always made me not restless, but apathetic—but also waiting to see if the physicians' advice might eventually prove to be correct and the place turn out to be less imperfect than it seemed.

Every evening from five to seven, I sat on the main terrace of the hotel overlooking the lake, keeping to my place under the wooden window boxes of geraniums. I had arranged my time carefully; it is my custom to arrange my time carefully and to follow my schedule exactly. I broke each day up into a number of almost identical segments that, by their abiding uniformity, never gave me the impression that time was passing either too rapidly or too slowly.

Every morning I took as lengthy a walk as I could manage in the woods, lunched generally in some restaurant in the town, and returned to the hotel for a long siesta in my room with the shutters closed. After a bath I remained for the rest of the afternoon on the terrace looking over the lake with a cup of tea or a drink, my inhaler in my lap in its zippered bag, a book or the newspaper or sometimes nothing at all, just the changing light in the leaves to amuse me.

Of course, at night, at times, there were men—not the type who could cause one any trouble.

As for this one, the one who came over to me on the terrace of the hotel, he said, I believe, after some preliminary excuses for the disturbance he was causing, "Were you not related to Daisy Summers?" or perhaps "You were a friend of Daisy Summers, it seems to me?" or something of that sort.

I do not pretend to reproduce the man's vernacular. I did not pay sufficient attention to his words to render them with any sort of authenticity but can give only the general purport of what he said. He spoke, I believe, without any sort of elegance, but at the same time as a man of not a little education would speak and, as far as I noticed, with a slight accent that was familiar to me and immediately signaled the man as coming from the place I had left a considerable time ago.

I do remember the name he said, and the way he said that name, which was what made me glance at the man who was standing before me. There was something about the way he said the name, something almost tentative and tremulous that took me somewhat by surprise; it did not appear to conform altogether to the rest of the man.

Even then I glanced at him for only a second and went on doing whatever it was I had been doing before: just gazing or reading my book or sipping tea. The name, though I recognized it vaguely, meant nothing to me, and the man actually interested me even less, of course.

I do not have a clear recollection of the man's physiognomy. All I remember was that there was something vaguely somber about his presence: either it was the hair or the eyebrows or the eyes or the skin, or perhaps even the fact that the fellow was not particularly well shaven; whatever it was, there was some impression of darkness to the man, that is all I can tell you, never having bothered, then or later, to peruse his countenance with much interest. He had on a white, not entirely clean shirt, open at the neck with no tie but with the intimation of some sort of common gold chain around the neck and, beneath that, what I imagined might be one of those hairy chests, a shiny jacket, rather too broad in the shoulders and too narrow at the waist for my taste, a pair of dark tight trousers that might have been navy or black or even dark green, that revealed far more than I wished to see of the man's masculinity, and those shoes that squeaked, went on squeaking, as he shifted his weight.

But even then the chap did not remove himself but continued to hover there beside me, blocking my afternoon light and view of the lawns and the trees.

To remove the man's shadow, or because I could not really do otherwise and remain within the bounds of common courtesy, or finally, because of the name, or the way the man said the name, I motioned him to the chair opposite. It was all the invitation the fellow required. He seated himself with his back to the lake. Something about the manner in which he sat down, or perhaps it was more something not a little familiar about the way he held his head or leaned forward across the table—I cannot name expressly what it was about the chap as, naturally, I was not really according him any sort of attention at all—but still something did convey the impression that this was not the first time I had seen the man on the terrace; the fellow might have been there before; I might have seen him before.

As far as I remember, the chap launched into the conversation by asking me if I knew what had happened to the girl whose name he had already mentioned.

"What happened to whom?" I suppose I must have asked him and gone on watching the boats returning to the land with their sails folded about their booms after a day on the water.

At times it amused me to watch the boats sliding through the water at twilight, coming silently into the shelter of the harbor. There was something slow and peaceful about the way the hull of the boat sliced through the calm surface of the lake that satisfied me and distracted me from the presence of those mountains that towered over the place so somberly like a warning of disaster.

By that time of evening the water was a steel blue, the mountains were already dark. They loomed above us, I felt, almost menacingly.

I suppose I may have been saying something about the boats while the fellow was expatiating on this woman whom he called Daisy Summers—one of those conversations one engages in so frequently, you know what I mean, the kind that runs along parallel lines.

I made a summary attempt to fit the name to a face, but I did not exert myself unduly. I was still under the impression the man was employing a rather unimaginative pretext to come over to my table and strike up a conversation with me that I presumed he would relinquish—the conversation, that is—without much persuasion, to take up other more promising prospects. I suppose I attempted to keep the conversation, as the fellow seemed to feel obliged to converse, as indifferent as possible. I think I said, "We've been lucky this month with the weather, haven't we?" or some such comment, supposing the fellow would be pleased to follow my example.

The pink rambling roses that climbed along the wall of the terrace had already been covered over to protect them from the cold of the night. I remember wondering whether this protection was absolutely necessary, and why it was the hotel gardener considered these roses needed this particular manner of protection.

However, the fellow did nothing to ameliorate his position by going on to apologize at length and, as far as I can recollect, in the most unoriginal, fatiguing way, for this intrusion. He kept insisting that he had no desire to disturb me, that he was not accustomed to importuning solitary women, particularly attractive women, or perhaps he said elegant women, something of that sort, that he was aware it was really quite reckless of him, etc. etc., none of which I believed for a moment, naturally, and all of which did more than a little to exacerbate my annoyance. He continued to maintain, with exasperating insistence, despite the fact that I gave him no encouragement whatsoever, that he was quite convinced he had seen me with this girl, or that I was related in some way to this girl or had even been close friends with this girl he called Daisy Summers. Not only did the chap's words annoy me, but for a reason that was not apparent, they began to make me not a little uneasy.

However, I let him run on for a while rather as one does a horse that has bolted, you know, hoping he would eventually tire and come to a halt of his own volition, without any effort on my part.

I have often found this an excellent means of coping with bores, and how many people are there who are not bores? The world, of course, is peopled mainly with bores, is it not? I find it not unpleasant, though, just to sit back and relax, awash in a murmur of half-heard words, letting them ebb and flow like waves around me, my attention wandering where it will, whilst the other, the speaker, goes on, sails forth quite contentedly. It is extraordinary to what lengths people will go, without requiring any sort of encouragement. One can generally make out the ostensible meaning at some point or simply add a nod or an exclamation here or there, and no one is the wiser. I have always asked myself how people can possibly believe anyone would want to listen to all of that.

So I sat there, as I often do, hardly listening, or only listening sufficiently to follow the general purport of what the fellow was saying—going on with my tea, I believe, or perhaps I had already moved from tea to a gin and tonic with lime, and was only sensible really, to tell you the truth, of the light fading rapidly, the sun sinking and the mountains black above us, and of the fellow who had somehow shifted his weight as he talked, so that he was leaning rather uncomfortably close to me, breathing almost directly into my face.

"Hardly that," I said finally, in reference to this supposed close friendship or relation that he was so certain had linked me to this girl he called Daisy Summers. I unzippered my inhaler, pumped a couple of times, and repeated, "It could hardly have been that," in a somewhat exasperated tone at that point, wishing then to unburden myself of this importunate fellow. "That could only be a gross overstatement," I said, and commenced, I must say, to wonder vaguely why the wretched creature kept on about this business, whatever it was, and how I was to rid myself of him. I could not imagine how a man of this sort would have anything of interest to tell me about anyone and least of all about this girl, whoever she was.

I said, "Actually, I don't think I could really say I was close friends with anyone for that matter."

As far as I remember, that comment silenced him for a while, but still he did not move. We went on sitting there, on the terrace, under the geraniums—I have never particularly liked geraniums: too bright, too stiff, the sort of flowers one finds in the window boxes of Swiss banks—the fellow leaning half across the table with his shiny sleeve brushing my arm.

But even then he did not abandon the matter. After a pause, he renewed his attack. He asked me to attempt to consider where I might have made this girl's acquaintance, if I might not have been at school with this girl, or have met her, perhaps, at some birthday party even as a child. Would I not, he adjured me, with an urgency in his voice that struck me then as nothing but tiresome, because I was beginning to comprehend that the fellow was going to be not a little difficult to ignore, was not going simply to rise and dissolve into the darkening sky, nor was he going to settle for what it was that I had originally thought he was seeking, which, after all, would have been something I could have managed, could have understood, that I could have taken or left as I wished—would I not, he beseeched me, reflect carefully, and make absolutely certain that I had not even been at school with this girl? Could boarding school have been the place where I had made her acquaintance?

In an attempt to conclude the matter in some way that might be satisfactory to this fellow and thus shake him off, I did, perhaps, make some sort of an effort to place the name. I said, "Perhaps we were at school together. Maybe that's it. I suppose we might have been. The name is vaguely familiar. We might even have been in the same class at some point. I rather think we were. Perhaps she failed down into my class, or they put me up into hers. I really don't remember. It was a long time ago," and pulled my shawl—the black wool one with the red flowers embroidered along the edge—around my shoulders and snapped the flap of my handbag in preparation for my departure. I added, still hoping to change the subject and thus unburden myself of the loquacious fellow or at least this tiresome conversation, "The light is fading fast. Odd how it lingers and then suddenly gets dark, isn't it?" or something of that sort.

But the man refused to be put off. He still clamored

to know if I was able to recall what had become of this girl, as though it were possible that, not even remembering who she was, I could possibly have known or wanted to know what had happened to her.

"No idea. Whoever she is, I certainly haven't seen the woman for years," I said.

But even that reasonable statement did not satisfy the chap. He could not believe I had not read something about the matter in the papers somewhere or had not spoken to someone who would have informed me what had taken place.

I tried, summarily, to suggest that I had left all of that far behind me, that my existence out there might almost have belonged to someone else. I believe I said something like, "I haven't been back out there for years. I move around a great deal, you know. Never remain anywhere for very long. Quite lost touch with all of that. Always found that place dreadfully boring, myself. I prefer Europe these days. I have a place in the Cotswolds where I keep my things. This is rather a pretty spot, don't you think?"

It may have been then—but, of course, it is possible I am not remembering any of this in the order in which it actually transpired, particularly as I was hardly listening to the fellow, was according far more attention to the water and the mountains and even the bright, prim geraniums than to what he was attempting to tell me—that the fellow said he was certain he had seen me with this girl he called Daisy Summers at her place. He said something about my having spent a day with this Summers girl at her house. I remember this clearly, as the fellow repeated this supposition more than a couple of times. The fellow, as I remember, was the sort who repeated himself continuously, whether it was because the topic excited him particularly, or because this was his habit, I did not know, but I did know that his propensity to repetition added not a little to the general dreariness of his conversation.

He said something to the effect that he thought I might have visited this Summers girl's home, spent a day with her, and that he might have seen me there at that particular moment. I suppose I answered, "It is possible I visited her home once. I was often invited to the homes of my school friends, and sometimes I went. I might have visited these people you are talking about. I do have a vague recollection of a house, now that you mention it, and even some relatives who might have been hers, a mother, perhaps, or an aunt, perhaps more than one aunt, something like that. So I suppose it's possible you saw me there."

Then I made another, final attempt to silence the fellow. I was deadly bored by then, reduced to plucking off the petals from a flower and crushing the stem between finger and thumb to keep myself occupied—you can imagine. I attempted to rid myself of him entirely by assuring him that, despite all my efforts, I could not, in all sincerity, recollect another thing about this girl. I believe I told him, what was certainly the case, that I really did not have a very good memory for that sort of thing. I said, "Actually, I tend to remember things more than people. Anyway, one always remembers the most insignificant, the most useless of details and forgets the essentials, don't you think?"

This remark, however apt—and surely it was, in this case, particularly apt—seemed to have little or no effect on the man. I remember how he sat there: by then the man's face was so close to me I could hear the sound of his breathing. He breathed audibly with his lips open on the dark of his mouth. I was left no recourse but my inhaler, which I extracted once again and pumped.

I said, still trying to be courteous—I believe good manners are probably the most serviceable of all the virtues—but by then almost prepared to rise and leave the fellow sitting there in his shiny jacket and his squeaking shoes, "You know it really is getting rather late. I remember so little about this woman. I am honestly trying to tell you everything I know, but I don't think I can help you at all. I may have spent a day with her, it's quite possible, I do remember something about that house. She may have asked me to come and spend the day with her, and she may even have talked to me, told me the story of her life—heaven knows what she might have told me. But I really have no recollection of what she said, or what I might have said, or what I might have done. It was a long time ago, and besides, none of us listen much to one another, do we? In my experience, people just do not listen. They may even ask questions, but they don't listen to the answers."

But even this had apparently little issue. The man's tenacity was beyond my comprehension. I could in no way understand what it was the fellow was seeking with his incessant questions and his continuous flow of words. Of course, I had no notion, nor did I particularly care what the man was after with me. I had only one thought at that moment, which was, as it is with a fly that buzzes against one's face in the night, to unburden myself of the garrulous fellow.

Unbelievably, he continued to expatiate on this girl, though I can hardly recount what it was he said to me. I believe there was some question of a name. The fellow seemed not a little anxious to know if this Daisy Summers had mentioned the name of someone, perhaps some man she might have been involved with or something of that sort. All of this was interspersed in a most confused and irrational way with various odd bits of information about the man himself. I believe he actually attempted to tell me something about his own life, his father, his profession or his lack of a profession, what he was doing up there in the mountains, but, naturally, I paid no heed to any of that at the time.

As far as the name was concerned—the name the man thought this girl might have mentioned—I told him I had never been very good with names. I said, "My goodness, I even had difficulty introducing my own mother."

Finally, I told the fellow that it was the time that, in the normal course of things, I went in for my dinner, that I found it wiser not to eat at too tardy an hour, and that I liked to help myself to the hors d'oeuvres before anyone else attacked them. On Sunday evenings the hotel usually served a buffet dinner, and I presume this must have been a Sunday evening.

By then I had almost forgotten the fellow, who had slumped again into silence, sitting in the rapidly fading light. I was thinking about the amazing quantities of food people took from buffet tables, the way they heaped up their plates, and how they contrived to consume all of that. Perhaps I told the chap that, personally, I found the whole business of eating rather a bore. I could never decide what to eat, particularly in that place where the choice was generally between a *bifteck, pommes frites* and a *bifteck, pommes frites*.

He said suddenly—I suppose he may have been contemplating my face, or what he could see of my face in that dim light—I remember this quite clearly, "You know, you look like her. You really do. There's definitely something about you that makes me think of her. There's some resemblance."

I replied, "I look like whom?" When he had made it sufficiently clear that he was still talking about the same girl, I suppose I replied that I could not imagine why he considered I resembled this Daisy Summers, though, to tell you the truth, I had great difficulty conjuring up her features at all. The only sense I had of the girl's face was that it was quite probably a most ordinary one, a face, as far as I could recollect, without any sort of distinction at all.

To which, I believe, he said, "You have the same fair skin that burns easily."

I said abruptly, with the desire that this would close our discussion, "It starts to get cool at around this hour. It is really rather chilly this evening, don't you find? It is definitely time for me to go in to dinner. Please excuse me now."

But the fellow's expansive presence did not undergo any sort of contraction. He could not let me go. He only crushed the book of matches he held in his hand and went on sitting there. I was beginning to feel the fellow was as immovable as the mountains above us. He implored me for just a minute of my time. He was still quite convinced that I might be able to remember something. He seemed quite unable to let the matter lie and to rise and leave me to go in for my dinner.

After that I hardly listened to what the man said, and it was only an inherent sense of propriety that kept me sitting there at all. I heard but barely registered what the man was saying. At the time I was aware only that he became most insistent, and that a flood of words issued from him. Afterward I was able to recollect some of what the man said to me, but at the time, I paid little attention to his words. Afterward, I was to remember more than I cared to remember of the man's words. But that was later.

Finally, as I was about to rise while the man was rambling on in this almost incoherent manner of his about the moments he had spent with this girl and about how young and foolish he had been, about the importance of my recollecting or the importance of his knowing or even the consequence to the general public of my remembering whatever it was he was begging me to remember, what this woman had said, or some name this woman might have mentioned, or something of that sort, the fellow placed his hand on my arm—I suspect in his eagerness to retain me—as he told me, what I actually knew by then anyway, that someone must have done away with this woman in mysterious circumstances.

It was not possible for me to get up then; all I could do was to pull my shawl about my shoulders and cross my arms and watch the rambling roses along the wall, lit by the light from the dining room within, under the netting that covered them over against the cold of the night. I was obliged to remain there for a moment at least; it would hardly have been appropriate to depart immediately.

I sat for a while in silence, staring at the flowers and then, my eyes drawn upward despite myself, staring at the mountains, whose darkness had become one with the dark of the night. Though even the outlines of the mountains had vanished, could only be imagined, felt, the night was full of their ominous form. I sensed their presence huddled over me, the sensation of foreboding they inspired conglomerated, gathered force in their physical absence.

I was suddenly quite overcome with hunger and fatigue, wearied by this man's insistence, bored by his presence, or simply by the duration of time I had remained in the same place. I had been exposed for too long. The night had grown cool. The mist had risen from the lake. For a moment I shivered. I was afraid I might have caught cold, sitting out in the damp evening air.

Then, too, something else occurred that I suppose I might mention. I was aware that the man had moved, had somehow taken my wrist, had his hand on my wrist, was holding, gripping, not my hand but my wrist. His cheeks, as far as I could see in the gloom, had reddened, his eyes had brightened, and he appeared to me to be perspiring slightly; beads of perspiration clung to his forehead, and his dark hair was not a little damp around the hairline.

I let my arm lie in his hand. I looked down at the man's hand. He had long, fine, blunt-tipped fingers, deft, strong, agile hands, hands that were very clean, the nails carefully manicured. He wore a diamond ring set in gold on the little finger. The ring seemed too small for him. His hands, like the manner in which he said the girl's, Daisy Summers', name, surprised me; they did not seem to accord with the rest of the man.

It crossed my mind then that one might sleep with this man or not sleep with this man and that it would come to exactly the same thing.

I rose and left the man sitting there.

The dining room seemed particularly lugubrious to me that evening. It was a large room that led off one of the lounges and looked over the lake. At that hour, though, the heavy green velvet curtains were drawn across the windows and billowed gently in the evening breeze. The whole room, for some reason, I thought, resembled some underwater region.

The lime-green walls seemed to me to cast a sickly glow, accentuated by the discreet lighting of the small, shaded table lamps, so that even the white tablecloths and the limp, pink carnations in their silver vases, reflecting the green, glowed, seemingly phosphorescent. The potted palms in the corners of the room, I thought, appeared to fold and unfold the fingers of their leaves in the slight breeze like sea anemones.

Only a very few people huddled over their soup, wrapped in the anonymity of their age and wealth. There was almost no sound in the room as though, I imagined, the pervading gloom had silenced the guests. Besides the waiter's discreet murmuring and the scrape of silver on porcelain, there was nothing to be heard.

I sat at my table, wondering why on earth the walls had been painted such a ghastly green. I am not a little sensitive to colors, and the green discommoded me particularly that evening. The duck, which I had ordered, was definitely a mistake, and even the bottle of wine I had selected, a not inexpensive bottle of Dole, was not enough to muffle my mood.

My encounter with the importunate man on the terrace and the fate of the barely remembered girl he had spoken of had almost entirely slipped my mind. I was certainly not thinking of either of them, but the stillness of the place, which I generally did not notice, or even welcomed, unnerved me.

I looked around the room, suddenly struck by the absurdity of it all—the shining silver, the ridiculous tubular flower bowl on each table, the half-dead, drooping carnations, each object in its well-chosen place, all the apparent solidity of a supposedly well-organized world. For a moment the whole room seemed to waver slightly, to quiver, and an absurd thought crossed my mind: I thought I heard the sound of the fellow's crepe-soled shoes on the parquet floor.

I was even drawn, for some unaccountable reason, to exchange a few pleasantries with my neighbor in the lounge after the meal over a cup of coffee, something I had naturally never done before, a ridiculous elderly woman whom I had always shunned, who dined alone and arrayed herself in the same absurd black taffeta hat every night for dinner and generally slipped a couple of oranges into her knitting bag, surreptitiously, before retiring.

In my room I reclined on my bed and actually smoked a cigarette. I had given it up—cigarette smoking, that is—years before, naturally, with my complaint, but I always keep a pack of filter-tipped Dunhills at hand for emergencies such as this one.

I lay there with only the bedside lamp lit, inhaling, drawing the smoke deep into my lungs, savoring the nicotine and the thought of what it was doing to my lungs, voluptuously—it was of course strictly against the physicians' orders—I even followed the cigarette with a stiff, neat whiskey. A bottle of that, too, I keep in my chamber for medicinal purposes. I remember thinking that I had no desire, anyway, to continue living for as long as these same physicians would have liked me to continue living and to go on paying their bills.

I stubbed out my half-finished cigarette and attempted to read, but with little success. I was unable to concentrate.

What I was remembering as I lay there smoking was the dormitory at school, the light in the dormitory at school.

I could see then that in the dormitory the light was silver. The moon lit the room. The mosquito nets that hung from the row of narrow beds were drawn back, gathered into thick coils at the heads of the beds. Someone had smuggled an orange into the room from dinner, and the orange, or rather the skin of the orange, perfumed the air. It was very hot, although the windows were thrown open. I do not know what season it was. The seasons out there are hardly seasons. They change fast with no twilight pauses, no melancholy autumnal moments or gauzy spring promises. Summer slips into winter almost imperceptibly. It is always more or less hot and more or less humid.

The girls stood on the beds and threw a pillow from bed to bed, giggling, bouncing, waving their arms wildly, their locks flying, bending over to clutch their hollow stomachs in silent laughter, whispering in loud, hoarse whispers. If anyone dropped the pillow, she removed an article of clothing. That was the rule of the game.

The girl was wearing little clothing from the start. She jumped up and down on the bed, her half-formed breasts naked, her puerile body tight in her moist skin and silver in the light of the moon. I threw the pillow high and hard, so that she reached for it, her arms flailing the air. She fumbled, she teetered, and she almost fell.

It was somewhere around ten o'clock, I think, when the telephone rang. I was not really surprised, I suppose, to hear the man's voice.

As I remember it, he began once again by apologizing,

but I cut him short at once this time and simply asked him what he wanted. There was a pause. The chap begged to see me again.

I hesitated a moment, considering. I stood with the receiver in my hand, gazing at the bowl of red roses that stood on the dressing table, twelve red roses sent by some admirer, their heads drooping and a fine coating of slime lining their stems. I am not certain why I then said what I said, but it may have had something to do with the flowers. I told the man I had met on the terrace that if he wanted to see me to obtain additional information about the woman he had been expatiating on all that afternoon, he was wasting his time.

At long last he made his intentions clear.

To be absolutely certain there would be no mistake, I told him he might come to my room, but that my expectation was that he would not linger beyond a certain hour. I told him it was my custom to retire early, which was not an untruth—it is my habit to retire early with a book, not even answering my telephone after a certain hour. In this way, I thought, I would eschew any other lengthy conversations. As it turned out, I succeeded—the man said hardly more than a few words—but I was not prepared for the words he said.

By the time the man had arrived at my door, I had bathed, perfumed and powdered my body, and had already partly dressed. This was not particularly for the man's benefit but simply a ritual I always performed before any such encounter. Such rituals, I find, are what enable one to continue through life, though there are times when they seem almost too much effort to perform. I had perfunctorily brushed out my hair and let it lie loose about my shoulders, not out of any sort of coquetry, but so that the hairpins I use for my chignon would not press into the back of my neck. I was already feeling fatigued with all of this unaccustomed activity and beginning, as is so often the case, to regret ever having summoned the man to my room, when he rang my doorbell.

I cursorily inspected myself in the full-length mirror in the bathroom. I was attired, I believe, in nothing much more than my short pink silk shift—not the black one—and my black sandals.

As an adolescent I was sometimes under the impression I was too tall and too thin—all arms and legs and eyes. My stepfather, a military man who finally received his just deserts, kicked in the head by a horse—though there were moments when I thought that even this end was too quick and painless for the man and that I might have relished seeing him lie and suffer for a while—spent his time informing me, amongst other things of this sort, that I was too tall and that above all my feet were too large. Consequently, I stooped, acquired a sour expression, and wore shoes that were too tight for me and pinched my toes.

However, the advantage of such a figure—I am talking about my figure, of course—is that with the years—I am not, naturally, going to commit the indiscretion of telling you my age, but leave you to come to some reasonable conclusion on your own—there is not much flesh to sag or fall. I think I can say, without any vanity, that I have retained a deceptively youthful appearance, in certain kind lights. I always say, past a certain age, women should come out only at night. At any rate, what I saw in the looking glass that night, while the man was knocking on my door—I let him cool his heels out there for a while—did not entirely displease me.

I noticed too, with some relief, that the man, when I finally allowed him to enter my room, had changed his shirt to a clean one of some rather more attractive, transparent material and smelled of some not unpleasant eau de cologne. He was, however, wearing the same shoes, though I noticed he must have given, or had them given, a polish, but they continued to squeak as mournfully as ever as I let him lead me across the room to the bed.

The maid had removed the bedcover, and I had lit the bedside lamp—I like to see what I am making love to, naturally. I let the man commence the proceedings without any further preliminaries.

It was as we were both sprawled across my bed, and were already somewhat in disarray, that the man spoke of the fly. The fellow, as I remember, was reclining beside me, or rather against me, hardly even as clothed as I was. I believe he had on nothing more than the gold chain he wore about his neck, which swung back and forth in the hair on his chest. He had risen up on one elbow so as to gaze down at me, or rather to watch his hand, I suppose, and my body while he was touching my body.

He was not unschooled in the art. I allowed him to work his way freely from my upper extremities to the lower, which he accomplished with not a little ease, his hand maneuvering craftily with the straps of my shift so as to expose as much flesh as he was able, going on deftly with some method and some skill, lingering in the appropriate places, doing nothing in too hurried a fashion, nor loitering for too long, his touch sufficiently strong without being rough. I remember thinking that the fellow would have known how to shampoo the hair excellently, that his touch would have been just the thing for a really good shampoo, that it was a shame I could not think of some way to put him to shampooing my hair. As he touched me I let him press his swollen member against me or rather against the remaining thin silk of my shift that was all that still divided us, and which I had allowed him to work down and up to cover nothing much more than my waist and buttocks.

I reclined with my hands folded under my head and my gaze on the ceiling—there was quite a pretty molding on the ceiling of that room—letting him touch me—his caresses were not unpleasant, after all—but with not a little disinterest, permitting him to go through the motions. I was certainly in no way aroused by his hands or his body—there was nothing arousing about the fellow.

There was nothing actually wrong with the body, which was tanned for that time of year, broad-chested and slim-hipped, and the legs were really not unshapely but rather too short, I felt—he was probably an inch or so shorter than I am—and I've never been one, though I know there are some who do, to appreciate that much dark hair on the chest.

At this point in the lovemaking, if you could call it that, when I was beginning to wonder whether it would be worth continuing with the whole business, or if it would not be wiser to terminate the proceedings with some pretext—a sudden stomach cramp or nausea, or even a qualm of conscience, a husband I had not mentioned, perhaps, who could be offered up at the last minute to extricate me from the final act—when, without any apparent reason, and without slowing down in any way the movement of his hand or ceasing to caress whatever it was he was caressing at that moment, the fellow made that remark about the fly.

But she would never have hurt a fly.

I believe that was what he said. I am not absolutely certain of his words, but what I am certain of is what occurred while he was saying those words.

I remembered something about the girl he was talking about, the girl he called Daisy Summers.

The girl was in a large sunlit room with two or perhaps three beds. I saw her, this Summers girl, from behind, bending down, squatting on her haunches at first and then actually getting down onto her hands and knees and scooping at a small, black spider—a button spider, I believe they are called—pushing a stiff piece of white paper against the carpet, chasing the spider with a piece of white paper, chasing it along the edge of the mauve carpet onto the parquet floor again and again, turning the paper as it ran one way and then the other, until she caught it on the edge of the paper and ran to the window to liberate the creature. She threw open the window with one arm and the spider out into the creeper with the other, and turned to face me. The bay window that gave onto the garden was open, and the wind whipped the loose sleeves of her dress against her arms. I saw her sleeves flapping against her arms in the wind from the open window. That was what I perceived more distinctly than anything else: the wide, loose sleeves of the dress. Certainly I noticed the sleeves more than the face or even the body, though I cannot tell you exactly of what stuff the sleeve was made: something soft like shantung or crepe de chine or silk of some sort, something almost transparent, flapping, beating against the arms.

While I let the man go on touching my body, his hands descending into the inmost recesses, I was seeing this girl he called Daisy Summers, standing in the early morning sunlight with the bay window open behind her. I could see her quite clearly, almost as though magnified by memory: her arms and the sleeves of her dress flapping gently against her skin; I could see the blond hair on her plump, rounded arms and the pale freckles in her honey-colored skin. For some reason the memory aroused me.

I was enjoying the man.

It was only when the fellow had departed that it occurred to me that he had never mentioned his name. All that evening he had been saying the name of this Summers girl, but he had never told me his own.

When the man had gone, I rose from the rumpled bed and let my eyes wander over the things scattered about me. I walked about arranging the room, remaking the bed carefully, emptying the ashtray and putting the glass away, actually wiping the trace of his shoes from the parquet floor—I cannot abide any sort of disorder—and touching my things: my books: the Austen, the Henry James, the Naipaul, and the Virginia Woolf; the silver brush and comb set; the photo of Mother, as a young woman, in its silver frame; the cut glass bowl; the petit point cushion; my rings; the cameo broach; the unguents for my toilet; the clothes in my closet; my numerous suitcases and the straw bag I used on my walks. Somehow the room looked bare to me, as though something were missing. It even occurred to me that the man might have actually stolen something from me, but when I checked, nothing had been removed.

I took a long shower and scrubbed my skin with a

loofah, dusted and perfumed my body, creamed my face. I felt a sudden need for air. I crossed the room, opened the window, and stood there taking in great, deep breaths of night air. I realized that a light rain was falling. I could hear the sound of the rain dripping into the gutters and smell the damp earth. The weather had changed.

I gazed up at what I knew were the mountains, trying to discern their form in the mist and the dark of the night. There was no moon visible over Gerzett, not even a lone star in the sky. The heavy presence of the mountains, unseen, was suddenly quite intolerable. I sensed an attack of my complaint coming on; a sudden breathlessness overwhelmed me; I reached for my inhaler; I shivered and began to cough. I was certain I was feverish. I had caught cold. I had been heedless, remaining at such length on the terrace that evening, talking to a stranger, and then standing before the window in the damp night air after a hot shower. I knew all too well how dangerous a cold could be for someone with my illness. I wrapped myself hurriedly in a gown and climbed into bed, but I was unable to sleep. As I lay there tossing back and forth, alternately burning with heat and then shivering with cold through what remained of the night, that absurd notion came to me again: it seemed to me that I could still hear, would go on hearing, in the rustlings and heavings, in the creaks and the muffled cries, in all the anonymous sounds of the night, the man's crepe shoes squeaking.

What happened during the next few weeks one could, I suppose, attribute to the fever that kept me tossing in my bed, restlessly seeking a cooler place, under the illusion that the coolness of the sheets could assuage the heat of my body and the aching of my head; or alternately one might ascribe my condition to the inclement weather. It continued to rain each day, or seemed to me to continue to rain, after that, endlessly, that soft, monotonous drizzle, the kind of rain that has an almost hypnotic effect, or anyway produced that effect on my feverish mind; or again one might even maintain it had been provoked by the thick mist that rose and settled in what seemed to me a gray band, covering both the mountains and the lake, so that a traveler arriving in that place at that time would have believed the mountains and the lake simply a myth. The mountains, invisible, their imagined shape somehow steeper, rockier, even more bereft of any sign of life than their reality, in my not a little disturbed mind, were even more oppressive, and provoked an almost overwhelming sensation of suffocation in my constitution.

I admonished the physician, who was in almost daily attendance on me, and who afterwards sent me a dreadful bill for his services—a certain Dr. Constance, a pompous little Swiss man whose rotund shape and ruddy face leaned over me alarmingly during my bouts of fever—to let me depart from the hotel.

In my feverish state, I somehow associated that place, those mountains, that mist, the constant sound of the water dripping into the gutters, and even that dilapidated hotel, with its lime green walls, with my illness. I was convinced that if I could only rise and descend into the valley, I would be cured. I had a great longing for the lush cool of the valley.

At times I was under the impression that I was lying in the deep shade of tropical trees that hung over white sand. In my dreams, the dripping of the water from the pipes was transformed to the soothing sound of waves breaking on sand. The translucent waves were very clear to me, rising from the end of the whiteness of my bedcover with a curve and a crash, green-white and foam-tipped; I attempted to retain their coolness in my mind. The sea came to me through the mist of my illness, vast, immeasurable, eternal.

At some point during my illness—I had long since lost all idea of time—I was alarmed by something that produced a sensation that perilously skirted such a sharp shock, from the extreme quality of its unexpectedness, that I was almost brought to a swoon. It was, I believe, one evening, or at any rate the lamp was lit by the side of my bed. I woke suddenly from a fitful sleep to sit up straight, completely roused, certain of a presence at the side of my bed.

It was the presence of a dark figure that I was immediately aware was not the physician or the maid who came to adjust my bed or even the waiter who brought me the broth and zwieback I was unable to consume. I took this mysterious figure to be that of the man I believed I had met on the terrace. For some reason, the idea of his, after all, quite ordinary presence, appearing suddenly beside me as I lay there so helplessly, provoked some childlike irrational fear in me, and I could not bear to look upon what I took to be this man. I was not so much terrified by the shape of the man as what I took, in my delirious state, to be hiding behind the man, as though he brought in his train some sort of monster that crouched behind him and was bound to devour me. The monster was associated with the darkness of his countenance and the sound of his shoes. It was the sort of irrational fear that made me turn from this dark apparition to the wall in horrified silence.

When, coming sufficiently to my senses and daring to turn back toward this figure, I realized that it was only my neighbor from the dining hall, the elderly bore with the ridiculous black hat, I was filled with such a sense of relief and looked upon this absurd creature with such gratitude for being simply who she was, that I found myself even reaching out to grasp her knotty, age-spotted hand.

I believe—though this whole period is so confused in my mind that I am not certain of any of the facts I advance here—I proceeded to order her, too, to help me rise and leave that chamber and even made some desperate attempt to step forth from my bed. The silly creature rushed for Dr. Constance, who, naturally, would not hear of any such project and, instead, prescribed even larger doses of cortisone and absolute rest.

Perhaps the odd turn taken by my mind could be attributed quite simply to the cortisone. Whatever it was, during that period, my mind returned continuously to the memory the man's words had inadvertently aroused, the figure of this woman he called Daisy Summers.

Not that I was preoccupied, obviously, by the thought of her death or her life, or anxious in any way to discover what had become of this girl, or why she had died—this girl was nothing to me. I remembered nothing about her except this one memory that the man's words had evoked, and the name that was vaguely familiar. Nor was my mind preoccupied by the man on the terrace, or even by why the man on the terrace had questioned me with such insistence about this Summers girl. He was, after all, a man who had really not interested me in any way, not someone of my own class, nor did he have any of the physical attributes that might have redeemed his lack of breeding, though the man, or rather the sound of his shoes and the dark something about his countenance, had become in some way vaguely and quite unaccountably threatening to me. But my mind, even in its feverish state, was hardly concerned with such matters.

I was, rather, assailed, despite myself, for some reason I was utterly unable to grasp, by what I could only consider as the amazing recurrence of this initial memory, always the same memory: this girl, bending down to save the life of a spider and then standing before the open window in the sunlight with her sleeves flapping in the breeze.

The memory became as fixed in my mind as the flickering, faulty shapes of some early film, the black and white forms blurred and indistinct in certain places but in others still a most exact and detailed replica, though obviously no such moving forms existed. Who would have bothered to film so insignificant a moment?

Besides, I was certain of one thing—no one had seen this woman at this moment but myself and God.

THE ISLAND

I was not really listening to her, because I was watching the ornate silver brush she clasped in her hand, or, through the half-drawn curtains, the mauve jacaranda blossoms, floating down slowly to the ground. I was gazing out the window at the green lawns, reaching out like a hand to the distant, gray-blue hills, and the blossoms, floating down so slowly, caught in the breeze for a moment, so that they seemed to drift upwards, not downwards, as though they had a life of their own, as though they were lifted up by hope, buoyed up, before they fell to the ground. Naturally, I did not hear her words.

She was not the sort of person whose words could have possibly had any interest for me, you can imagine—not anyone who had any of the qualities I could have possibly admired: an ordinary girl in every way, even when she was telling me that dream, above all when she was telling me that dream about drowning.

Besides, I was used to letting my mind wander when people started telling me this sort of thing, or what I thought was this sort of thing. I went on looking out the window.

Even when she turned to me, grew quite insistent, clasped the brush in her hand, the sparks flying from her hair, I did not really accord any attention to what she was saying. I continued to gaze out the window.

It usually brings people to a stop, eventually—ignoring them, I mean—if all they desire is just someone to listen to them, which was not what she desired.

Afterward, in the bamboo shoots, it was not possible to ignore her, though I was aware, I suppose, that I could have stayed or left. It did not seem to make much difference.

The wind never dies on this island. At times, you might think it had died, but if you look carefully enough you can see that the very tips of the trees are still trembling. Then it begins again its constant wuthering, sweeping the clouds from the sky, scattering sand, lashing at the stunted pines, stinging faces, legs, and hands, moaning through the night.

They have different names for the wind here: they call it the sirocco, the warm wind that comes from the deserts of Africa, or the mistral, the colder wind that blows from the north, and other names I do not recall. They say it lasts one, three, or nine days, but they do not tell you it never quite dies, it goes on blowing incessantly.

The island seemed to me, in a strange way, like a memory I could not quite grasp. It was, still is, an exposed, barren place. The sun-dried earth stretches before one as monotonously as the still, glittering sea. Only stunted pines and gray-green juniper bushes grow in sheltered places. Almost nothing of the various peoples who have conquered and pillaged the land through the ages remains except for the stone walls that originally divided the shepherds' land, an occasional ruined shepherd's hut, and those heaped piles of reddish stones they call *nuraghi*, whose origin has been puzzled over for centuries but remains mysterious.

The sun shines almost constantly, and the water is a calm, clear, turquoise blue. It was the water and the light that particularly pleased me, that familiar, brilliant light that causes the stone walls to cast dark shadows.

When I had finally convinced Dr. Constance to allow me to leave Gerzett and the mountains, I proceeded southward, stopping only to rest in various anonymous, and for the most part rather dreary, hotel rooms, chosen at random from an old guide book. Once I had the crossed the border from Switzerland into Italy, the particular impression I received, though, was of someone turning on the color, just as in some children's film one section is sometimes set off from the other by this rather obvious device. I had the notion I had come from a black-and-white region into a multicolored one.

The traveling, though almost constant, seemed strangely beneficent to my health. I breathed more easily.

I pumped less. My lingering cold lifted. The mohair blanket I had kept wrapped about my knees or my shoulders was stowed away in one of my numerous portmanteaus. I have a not inexpensive taste for good luggage, and a fairly considerable collection of monogrammed leather suitcases follows me wherever I go.

My mind was pleasantly vacant. I thought only of practical details: when trains ran, where to find a porter, where I would stop or not stop for the night, where I would dine, where I might obtain a book or a newspaper, what it might be necessary to unpack or what would be quite as convenient to leave in my suitcase, what I would need to launder by hand or what I could simply fold up, place in plastic, and ignore for the while.

I am an excellent packer. I would even go as far as saying that packing is my strong point. I am able to fit quite a considerable quantity of heterogeneous garments—I like to travel in comfort, naturally—into a rather reduced area. The trick, I have found, is to lay everything just as flat as possible; this prevents creasing and enables one to arrange a considerable quantity of things in a very compressed fashion.

Oddly enough, for someone who has never really delighted in traveling, the movement and even the sound of the trains I found not a little soothing. I discovered that I rested better than I had done in the mountains. I even liked the manner in which the trains halted suddenly in the night in some small, unknown station for no apparent reason, and the deep perfect silence that ensued.

The passing landscape was quite sufficient to amuse me. I sat gazing out at the countryside: at scintillant green hills, brilliant bushes of forsythia, terra-cotta–colored facades of farmhouses. The man on the terrace slipped from my mind as though I had never set eyes on him, and with him vanished the woman he had spoken of as though they were in some way intimately connected, bonded, of the same flesh.

The town where I finally stopped was an artificial place, anonymous in its cleanliness. Newly whitewashed identical houses lined the sides of gray-green cliffs; quiet, scrubbed streets were shaded with well-watered oleander bushes, their leaves shimmering in the sunlight. The few people there at that time of year—it was still relatively early in the season—came from everywhere: Milanese, Arabs, Germans, and an occasional Englishman. They all looked more or less alike, as far as I noticed, as though they might have been related in some way: all slender, all tall, all opulent, all golden brown.

I sometimes stood at the window of my room and glanced distractedly at the people parading across the piazza, but more often I gazed into the distance down to the sea. From my hotel window I could see the gray-green shrub-covered land, the azure sea and beyond that the sun-blanched sky, with only faint lines between them. I stood looking across the sea, the smooth expanse that might almost have been the water of a lake. There are no mountains in this part of the island, only the swell of the scrub-covered, rocky hills. I studied the hibiscus that grew by my window along the wall, that flower of hot places, the white hibiscus with the deep hollow of the petals shot with a purple that spread through them like a stain. The odor of the sun on some bittersweet herb, rosemary or sage or some herbage I was unable to name, mingled with that of the sea and scented the air.

I soon established a new routine to my days, taking the

early boat each morning from the hotel dock to a distant beach, lying on the sand watching the changing light on the water or swimming with a mask, gazing at the fragmented light flickering on the seabed, lunching at the hotel, taking lengthy siestas in the heat of the day, and spending the remainder of the afternoon and the evening in the cafe on the piazza overlooking the harbor.

It was because of the wind, to tell you the truth, because of the wind and perhaps also of the boat, that I allowed the German into my bed.

I am loath to dwell too long on the poor fellow and would hardly have alluded to him at all—the chap, the German chap, had no importance in himself, but his lovemaking, or rather his attempted lovemaking, played a rather curious role in my recollections.

I had been swimming, had probably swum farther than I should have, and had regained the beach with my knees somewhat shaky. The challenge that swimming presents to someone who suffers from my ailment amuses me, and I have always enjoyed such an activity. You can imagine with what exquisite suspense I plunged into the sea.

The water was a clear, turquoise blue, full of brilliantly colored fish, coral, sea anemones, starfish, and the shells discarded by sea urchins.

It was the shells I was seeking and not the fish. I made quite a collection of shells during my stay, filling a large glass bowl with what I gathered, diving down deeper and deeper, into the obscurity of the rock formations, hunting the rare, large purple shells, increasingly able to hold my breath for longer and longer periods.

That morning, I had covered a greater distance than

was my habit, forgetting myself as I swam, my senses dulled by the water, my attention occupied solely by my gazing down at the bed of the sea. But the thought that was gradually occurring to me was that I had swum not a little way from the shore, and that if I should have an attack of my malady at such a distance from the shore, it would almost certainly be the sort of attack to terminate things definitively.

I was thus somewhat relieved to have achieved my footing on the land. I rose from the water slowly, treading carefully, retrieved my white hooded robe and pulled it about me and stood there resting, leaning my head back, letting the wind dry my hair, looking at the almost, and sometimes completely, naked bodies—it is considered essential to wear as little as possible on that beach—stretched out in orderly rows, lined up on the sand, the brown, greased bodies prostrate in the sun, silent, immobile, eyes closed, arms by the sides, each one in its assigned place. They might almost have been dead, I thought.

It was then I caught sight of the German, who came striding toward me, eyes lit up, as though he was looking at something unsettling. He struck up a conversation with me on the beach that morning as I emerged from the water. I was shaking out my hair, panting a little, standing on the edge of the beach in the sunlight, my feet still in the sea, the drops of water falling down my back and shoulders. As is the custom in that place, I wore nothing under my white robe but a thin black string that covered the bare essentials.

I welcomed the distraction the chap brought after my lugubrious thoughts in the sea.

Quite frankly, despite the smocked dresses and the bows in the hair, I cannot maintain that my stepfather was entirely mistaken. I was probably not a winsome child. Perhaps I grew too rapidly. I suppose as I became older, I must have acquired a certain quality, something to do with the whiteness of my skin or the lightness of my eyes, that sometimes attracts a particular quality of person.

On that beach of bronzed bodies, the extreme pallor of my skin—did I mention that I'm very careful with my skin in the sun?—the very length of my limbs, the luster of my nails, which I always keep long and highly polished, perhaps even my immobility—I suppose I stood there hardly moving—may have been somewhat remarkable. At any rate, this German fellow was apparently interested.

He accosted me directly and said something rather absurd about not being quite sure I was real, about feeling obliged to come up and talk to me to make certain of my substantiality. He went on mumbling something about a dream, about my rising from the water like a dream. "I thought you might be an illusion," he added. He spoke the rather formal English foreigners speak and actually pronounced these words in all earnestness. Despite the preposterous formality, which is something one should mistrust, I have always found, I let the fellow go on, aware, of course, from the way he lowered his glance, that he was obviously far more interested in the shape of what one no longer needs to conceal on beaches like those than in any supposed insubstantiality.

What I noted, actually, were the perfectly white teeth that he exposed as frequently as possible in a flashing smile that uncovered far too much pink enthusiasm. He mumbled something in a low voice about the Snow Queen.

"What did you say?" I asked.

"Oh nothing, just a thought that came to me."

As he made this ridiculous remark, he lay his hand on my arm. I could feel him trembling. I was filled for a moment with something approaching vitality, a rather bizarre and heady impression of power that quite pleased me. I realized, you know, that the fellow was more or less at my mercy. Of course, it was not the first time I had encountered something of this sort. There had been other occasions. There was that teacher in boarding school, a maths teacher, I believe, a Miss B—what was her name?—something that began with a B.

It was just before the fall of night, and the stars were shimmering brightly in the pellucid blue of that vast African sky. The sounds of the girls' voices rose and fell in the darkling air. Miss B said, "I know we shouldn't. I know it's very rash of us. Let's hope no one's looking. We're bound to get rheumatism, but what a glorious night!" She giggled, all the horse teeth protruding, and strode down the stone steps and sprawled. She was a tall woman, big-boned, with stiff, long legs that made her appear to walk on stilts. She threw herself into the damp, harsh grass with something approaching abandon.

I vaguely remember some scandal concerning one of the teachers at school. There was an impropriety committed by one of the teachers that brought about her downfall, caused her to be banished ignominiously and eternally from those idyllic grounds.

As I remember her, she had pale blue eyes, large damp hands, and a white powdered face that still showed the traces of a severe case of the usual juvenile skin malady.

What I remember most clearly about the woman was her inordinate propensity to fill the air with a fine spray when she spoke, so that one was almost obliged to turn from her, to retreat, to take cover, when she began to talk. This infelicity brought the girls to her class one morning equipped for rain, complete with raincoats, boots, and umbrellas. We marched into her classroom and cowered before her, as though about to receive grapeshot flying forth from the cannon of her wide mouth. I have a feeling that this attire was probably instigated by no one else but myself.

But I digress. To return to the German, the ridiculous fellow wanted me to lunch with him at his hotel. He waved a muscular arm at his boat, not an insignificant vessel, anchored off the beach, and offered to accompany me to my hotel to change if I wished and then to his place for luncheon. I told him I always ate alone and attempted to dismiss him. You know, to tell you the truth, I have never enjoyed breaking bread with a stranger, or even with some people I know rather well. It is quite unbelievable how many people have bad table manners, is it not?

At any rate, finally, perhaps because the fellow persisted, or, more probably, because the wind had begun to pick up, was blowing again in gusts, sending the sand flying against my legs, the wooden parasols creaking and swinging, shadows moving on the sand, I told him he might take me back to my hotel and return after lunch to accompany me to the smaller islands in his boat. I wanted to visit the island called Mortorio.

The afternoon was torrid. Even the wind was hot: the sirocco, coming from Africa, carrying desert sand, so they said. It offered no respite from the heat. It started to blow before noon and gusted on and off during the afternoon and raged rather wildly, all through that night.

After my lunch I closed the shutters of my room and reclined in the bath, a little breathless in the half-dark and the heat of the water, alternately smoking and pumping, listening to the sound of the wind in the shrub, hoping the German fellow would at least be late.

The bath is one of the places I prefer, certainly not a place I leave readily, a place where one can close the door and remove oneself, put oneself in parentheses, as it were, from the rest of humanity. It is a place for reading and thinking, where one's mind wanders easily, where time seems temporarily suspended.

I like to recline in very hot water, the steam rising around me, so that I might be almost anywhere, letting the heat seep through me, you know, soothing the aches and, after a while, adding less hot water, so as not quite to fall asleep. I have sometimes read an entire book in the bath in this fashion, my fingers crinkling up completely.

The room was very still, the trapped air smoky. Only the motes of dust in a single beam of light moved.

I'm sure you were friends, good friends, best friends, or even relatives of some sort. I'm quite convinced Daisy and you were close in some way.

"I don't have any best friends," I suppose I replied.

Like some sleeping neighbor whose head keeps rolling tiresomely onto one's shoulder when jolted by the movement of a train, the man's words kept coming back to me. The man on the terrace in Gerzett kept repeating to me, all that evening, these words or some similar version of these words.

At the time, I suppose, I accepted this statement uncritically and with as much urbanity as I could muster. I doubt I asked the man what had brought him to this conclusion, or even who this girl was with whom I was supposed to be best friends.

The man on the terrace at the hotel in Gerzett had gone on at such length and so tiresomely that I had listened to little of what he had said. I heard but I did not listen. It was as if he had not unburdened himself for some time, or had not unburdened himself of this particular matter for so long, as if the sight of me had brought this business to his mind rather suddenly, so that the words gushed from him like a torrent that breaks its banks, or like a huge wave that throws up pebbles and sand as it rushes forward, or even a wound that, suddenly reopened, bleeds anew. I could hardly have listened to all of his words.

I realized then, lying in the bath, staring at the blue and white tiled wall, that this girl, this Summers girl, might have telephoned me or written me a letter. I decided, as I soaped myself carefully—did I mention that I always use French soap as I find it keeps its fragrance better than any other?—it was probably a telephone call. Almost immediately, however, the call slipped my mind. I was aware only that at the time of the call I had not been quite certain who was telephoning me, but naturally, I had little desire to think about that. I was still quite certain I knew almost nothing about this girl.

Besides, I was thinking of something else. If I half-shut my eyes, I could make the arabesque pattern on the tiled wall swell and then recede, almost as though the blue and white tiles were pulsing or breathing, had become animate. There was something slightly menacing in this movement.

For some reason, the cornflower blue of the tile brought to mind a dress of Mother's, an evening dress with a sequined bodice and a full net skirt. For a moment I could almost see the folds of the net skirt undulating, as Mother turned on her heels.

The material was brushing against my face.

There is not much I remember about Mother, and, have no fear, I have no intention of launching into a lengthy description of my childhood. Most people, I know, love to expatiate on their infancy, but I have little interest in mine. Why should I remember all of that? Still, for some reason I have a distinct remembrance of Mother's clothes. She had an extraordinary collection of clothes.

I realized then, as I lay in the warm bath in that steamy hotel bathroom with the pulsing tiles, that this Summers girl had actually telephoned me. I even remembered where I was when she telephoned. This I saw rather clearly—these things began to appear to me in flashes, often silent, half-obscured flashes, rather like the flickering light on the underworld of the sea, but moving pictures that gradually came to seem as real as the objects around me.

I realized then that when this girl called I had been in the bath at home, alone, and naturally, as was my habit, I almost let the telephone ring without answering it at all. I even remembered the feeling of annoyance, of having risen out of the warm water and the world of the book I was reading, to answer the telephone, only to discover it was someone I knew slightly, with whom I had no wish to converse and certainly no wish to hear what she was asking me to hear.

I was reading in the bath, the bath being, even in those days, in the days when I had just finished school or was just about to finish school, my favorite place to read.

Naturally, I did not recall the words of that conversation. After all, I was probably standing there with a towel around my waist and another around my shoulders. Even so, the water was dripping down my back. My mind was still on the book, of course, probably a book by Balzac, whom I admired at a very young age, delighting mainly in his descriptions of rooms.

I do not believe that, initially, I was even able to place the name. For a moment I was probably not quite certain which Daisy she was—after all, Daisy is not an uncommon name—or even if I knew a Daisy. It was only after she had repeated her name and added her surname that I realized there was something slightly familiar about the voice. She continued rather rapidly, I believe, apologizing for disturbing me, perhaps taking my silence for understanding or anyway, for some sort of acquiescence. I presume I said very little in reply to her apologies, trying to close the window so as not to catch cold, with the telephone hooked between my head and my shoulder, letting the towel trail on the floor to contain the pool of water that was spreading like a stain.

I was not sure, then, what this Summers girl told me on the phone that day. Besides, I became aware then that the telephone in the hotel room was ringing, had probably been ringing for a while. It was the German fellow. I picked up the receiver and told him to wait while I dressed.

I put on a gown and opened the shutters.

I leaned out of my window into the light. The wind appeared to have abated somewhat. The tips of the pine trees tossed gently. A shadow trembled on the stone wall. In the distance the sea was a smooth, lacquered blue-gray, but near the coast it became a transparent turquoise. The wind had swept every cloud from the sky and rendered the colors pure and bright. The outline of the islands was clear. The birds chirped, their calls separate, short, out of harmony.

It was a moment in the early afternoon when the light was at its most brilliant and the June sky a blazing blue. The sun shone with its full strength, undeniable, uncompromising. It penetrated the transparent water, striking the blanched seabed, searching out the smallest shell hidden in the hollow of a rock, shimmering on the sides of the tall stalks of wild grass.

Oh, it had nothing to do with the fellow himself, the German fellow, I do not believe, though, I must say, he was rather broad across the shoulders and chest and in other important areas, if you see what I mean.

He was not late but five minutes early.

I suppose I might as well describe the fellow to you now and be done with it. However, I promise not to bore you with a detailed account of his physique. It will suffice to say that he did not look poor. I suppose that was the first impression I had of him. He looked rich even in his bathing suit. It was something about the tan. He had a rich man's tan. He was slightly taller than I. He smelled of eau sauvage, and his blond hair was still damp and combed back neatly with a fall and a rise over the forehead.

I was wearing my white piqué dress, the one with the high waist and the short skirt that I had purchased during my stay in Milan. Not that I suppose the fellow was particularly interested in my clothes but rather, in what was underneath.

At that point what I was interested in, quite frankly,

was the boat. It was the kind with a motor and a skipper, and polished brass and wood, and thick cream cushions where one can recline in the sun. What I wanted particularly, which I alluded to before, I believe, was to visit the island called Mortorio. Someone had informed me there was a beach of red coral there, which had been worn down slowly by the waves and the weather until the sand had become quite pink. I believe the island was called Mortorio. I had not had the opportunity of visiting such islands, and a boat like this would provide the freedom to go to them.

There were moments when I felt the need to escape the island. I have never been adventurous, you know. I have always preferred the known to the unknown. I do not like surprises. Left to myself, without any illness, or physicians to advise me, I would probably have been sufficiently satisfied in my own damp abode in the Cotswolds. Did I mention that the place was once a monastery and is supposed to be haunted by irate monks, their land usurped in the time of Henry the Eighth? To tell you the truth, I have never seen anything vaguely resembling a ghost.

Besides, I have always preferred to have my own things about me and would have been rather content, not going much farther than a short stroll in the mist in my own garden, alone, with the dogs or the cat.

But recently I had become restless, and the German fellow, I thought, with his boat and with his enthusiasm, would make for the perfect escort for some sort of venture.

When we left, it was still early in the afternoon, I believe, and still very hot, the sun high and direct, the colors bright and clearly delineated. There was an amazing contrast to the light and shade in that place. The sun struck the sand hard and glittered on the water. The wind was low. We lay on the cushions of the boat and sipped wine. The fellow talked, I suppose, while I closed my eyes and felt the spray on my face and the gentle undulation of the waves.

I did not remember if this girl had said she was in serious trouble of some sort, or even if she asked directly for my assistance. What I did recollect was that during that telephone conversation she beseeched me to come to her house because of some matter that she claimed to be extremely urgent and that she insisted could not be discussed over the telephone.

Then, my memory of the conversation—what with the waves and the rocking of the boat and the German's white teeth, which he was wont to flash most disconcertingly—became very confused. Whether she said she desired me to come to her house because of something she wished to confide in me, or because of some advice she required, or because I was the only person that she esteemed could assist her with this matter, I could not ascertain, and I did not particularly care.

At this point you may very well be asking why I bother to recount all of this. Why on earth are you telling us about this girl whom you did not know well and did not want to know at all? you might say.

What was rather peculiar was, obviously, not this place, not this girl who was, even when all was said and done, quite an ordinary girl, but the thing I had forgotten. One would not really imagine, I suppose, that anyone would forget something of that sort. And what seems at least as peculiar to me was that after all those years I was to recollect what had come to pass. Of course, you might say that what I recollected was not what actually took place that day or was only some incomplete and half-borrowed series of events reflecting rather something I had perused somewhere, or you might even come to the conclusion that I had not forgotten as completely as I would have you believe.

Be that as it may, at that moment, I assure you, I was not remembering anything at all. I was stretched out languidly across cream cushions, observing the light on the water and in the distance the island of Mortorio, or what I took to be the gray-green shrub of the island of Mortorio under the glare of the sun. From time to time I glanced at the German, who was, I seem to remember, flexing his muscles, about to put on his gloves and to plunge into the water to go waterskiing. He was the sort of man who wore gloves, the kind without the fingers, when he went waterskiing.

I had a vague memory of an attempt on my part to extricate myself from the whole business with the invention of a series of excuses, probably including my illness, but obviously, in the end, I must have acquiesced.

It is sometimes the only way to handle a bore, though I could not then, or later, really imagine what this girl had said to oblige me and thus Mother to make that long, monotonous drive across the flat, charred fields and straight roads of the Highveld in the dusty heat. Not only was Mother an exasperatingly slow and somewhat distracted driver, but she smoked almost continuously as she drove, having me light her cigarettes with the car lighter before she snatched them from me, drawing hungrily on the filter tips and leaving the thick stain of her red lipstick on the gold, filling the air with smoke and me with nausea, until finally I was obliged to lie prostrate with my head turned into the shadows of the leather seat in the back of the automobile.

Perhaps I promised to go to this girl's place just so that I could replace the receiver and return to the bath before it got cold, though I am not certain if I did return to it.

At that moment I was studying the curve of the German's body as he leaned down toward the sea, the rainbow spray flying into the air around him, and I was not even attempting to discover what led me to go down from our estate to this girl's house, which was nearer the boarding school in the valley by the sea.

Perhaps, though, she promised some reward: a special repast, an outing—perhaps there was a boat at the Summerses', or even a gift. I may have been going down into that town to acquire some article of clothing or to visit a physician or the dentist before school commenced, or even to call upon someone else. Perhaps I wished to return to the Indian market, where I had bought the canary that I kept in a cage in my room.

At any rate, I gave the matter no more thought for the moment but concentrated on watching the waves and the color of the sea and the line of the German's body as he raced across the water.

As a matter of fact, in all of this—which one might call, I suppose, an account of a death, of the events that preceded it and of the place where it happened—I am convinced of very little. Very little, you know, was ever recorded in any official way. There was no trial, of course; no one, as far as I know, was questioned by the police; the family apparently assumed, or preferred to let it appear they assumed, it was an accident—people out there are wont to avoid scandal at any cost. Nothing much appeared in the papers, I presume, but then nothing much ever appears in the papers out there.

I cannot even give you a date as to when the thing took place. Figures have never been my strong point, and the life I have lived has not been conducive to any sort of chronological recording of events. I have never been the kind of woman, even as an adolescent, to keep a diary. The events of my life, or anyone else's, for that matter, never seemed of much interest to me and in any case not worth recording. Certainly, friendship, which never played much of a part in my life, has not been leavened with curiosity. Nor have I ever been obliged to preserve in writing or even to follow the rhythm of someone else's existence. I never married, you know, never felt the desire to link my life to someone else's, indefinitely. I never had any children. Nor have I ever had to work. My father left me a sum which has been quite sufficient to provide for my welfare.

About the people of that place I can tell you very little. Entre nous, I have never been particularly interested by people in any place. Besides, as I said before, I left all of that a long time ago. What I remember of the place comes mainly from a child's eyes. All I can tell you about those people is that they clung together with a certain rather maudlin solidarity—"*Agh, shame hey,*" they were wont to say, their eyes filling with tears at the sight of a child with a bow in her hair. Their doors were always thrown open to one another. They barbecued in the white sunlight. They sipped gin and lime by the sides of their tiled pools, the water slapping against the sides. They played bowls on carpet-smooth greens, bending down low in white dresses and white hats. They sang the Magnificat, eyes rolled back with self-satisfied sanctity. They rubbed white hands against white hands. They slung comradely arms around comradely shoulders. They threw heads back in shared laughter. They pushed, they pulled, they twisted, they turned, in too tight an embrace, shouting, scratching, shoving.

There was a lot of unspoken fear, for the future of the people in that place did not look particularly propitious at that time. They had faced bad times before, of course, and would probably face them again; however, most of them were still quite convinced of their inalienable rights and of certain simplistic rules that guided their actions.

Much of what I may tell you, of course, remains doubtful. In fact it is quite possible that the words I remember as this man's were not his at all, and the memories these words brought back to me might actually be inspired by something I have read somewhere.

Literature is considerably more interesting than life, I have always found. Certainly, though I always say lucidity is more valuable than sincerity, you can be quite sure I have not gone to the trouble of making anything up. It was all found somewhere, but where, Heaven only knows. Still, I might just as well go on as I began, so as to render this account somewhat realistic, biographical, or at least representative.

For some reason, while the German arched his muscular body in the spray, swinging from side to side across the wake of the boat, his shoulder almost touching the water, with the sun behind him, I kept hearing the voice of the man in Gerzett.

Surely you could not have forgotten that place completely, the trees—the royal palms in the driveway, the fish ponds, the sound of the sea. Something must have remained. I could swear I saw you there, at luncheon, or perhaps it was at tea.

Hell, there's no way I could have imagined someone like you.

I've a good memory for faces, and yours is not a face one would forget easily. I remember the color of your eyes—I've never seen eyes such a blue white. And the length of your nails. You had those very long nails even then, didn't you?

As far as this remark is concerned, and the others that I came to remember, I cannot, of course, assure you of its veracity.

I'd swear I saw you that day. Hell, I'd put my hand in the fire. You were sitting in the lounge, your legs crossed just that way—that gloomy lounge—sipping tea or not sipping tea. Didn't you refuse the tea, hey?

For this extravagant sally, I had, undoubtedly, no reply either. I received it with indifference. I cannot say that it surprised me in any way. I was not surprised by anything this man said, you know. But then, I am a person who is so little surprised. Nor did the man seem to expect any sort of answer at all. He simply continued.

Couldn't you even imagine a house that might correspond to this girl's house?

Surely you must remember those trees—such extraordinary trees—or the three old maids or at least the servants? Or were the aunts asleep that afternoon? Where were the aunts that afternoon?

"I'm not particularly endowed with that quality," I suppose I replied, referring to my imagination, and all the while thought: Thank God, imagination has never been my strong point.

Thank God I have always confined myself to facts. I was a moderately successful student, you know, though somewhat indolent. When I applied myself, I was capable of learning fast; I was lucid and able to organize material, but no one ever told me, thank God, that I was particularly endowed with what is generally called imagination.

But the man would go on, could not be stopped. I had no desire to remember his words. I had no desire even to remember the man, I assure you. He was really a rather common type with only those hands and that darkness of countenance to distinguish him from the ordinary members of the herd. No, I had no wish even to think about the man himself, let alone this girl he continued to mention. There was no reason for me to give a moment's thought to this girl. The girl was long since dead. Everyone has to get through the business of dying at some stage or the other, and it could be argued that it might be better to get it over and done with as soon as possible. And surely, how one died was not very important, after all? One kind of death or the other comes to much the same thing, provided the suffering is not long or particularly painful, of course.

At any rate, there was no justification for dwelling on this girl's death. It was not reasonable. It could even be dangerous. And I had no desire to think about this girl, who was less than nothing to me.

Still, there was no denying it. As I observed the German leaning to one side, almost touching the water with his body and waving at me with his free gloved hand and flashing all his white teeth, it was quite obvious to me that I must have visited this girl's place.

The rooms were still, musty places where the humid air remained trapped within thick, damp walls; the paint was peeling around the baseboards; nothing moved but the motes in the beam of sunlight that penetrated between the purple velvet curtains.

What I saw through the fragmented light in the spray, as the German swayed back and forth across the water, was this girl's place.

It seemed to me, then, doomed to disintegration, as evanescent as the spray that rose in the air. I had the impression all those carefully manicured flower beds, those shadowy delphiniums (was it delphiniums?) and the frail, fading, pink and white sweet peas, the white hibiscus, open to the sun; the trees, the mauve jacarandas that mingled with the flame of the flamboyants, the palms with their curved trunks ringed like the rounded arms of Zulu maidens; even that thick, harsh, resilient grass—I could smell the scent of newly-watered grass—all of that might turn instantaneously back to wilderness, and the country revert to its archaic state, leaving the land as it had been when the first men saw it.

They were not a pretty bunch, I suspect, probably a restless band of Bible-reading nomads, who grabbed what they could get, however they could get it, cut their way through that mysterious underbrush, the long grass and the indigenous strelitzia trees, their ragged leaves hanging down low over endless beaches, and hacked their way through bushes and clinging vines, the black and green mamba snakes coiled unseen in the branches of the trees, the space undivided, stretching out endlessly into the void of the sea.

Do not misunderstand me. I found nothing particularly interesting about this place—it was not an exciting place, not even a frightening place. After all, a rather dark and dreary house could hardly arouse much interest, could it? A square and—despite that impression of transience—a sufficiently solid edifice that stood on the side of a cliff, looking toward the sea, that might have been found, I suppose, anywhere in what was once the British Empire, could hardly inspire much interest. An old Victorian house with a corrugated iron roof and some kind of hanging trees, perhaps cassias, that arched over the roof, where the swallows or the sparrows or the finches or the Indian mynas—possibly it was Indian mynas, some sort of noisy birds, nested in the roof, the sort of raucous birds that rise up together in random gusts with the dry, sudden sound of beating wings, could hardly cause anyone to be afraid.

It was just a place that might have had nothing to do with me, that might have been part of someone else's existence, a somewhat yellowed photograph in someone else's album. It was in no way associated with any other recollection, let alone with any emotion I might have felt. It was just an isolated memory, or at the most a fragment of something else that had been utterly lost, part of something that might have come to me in certain rare and faceless dreams, something that had risen perhaps for a moment, evoked by a certain pattern of light and shade or the bitter sound of the rain, but always, before, sinking back down, almost immediately. It was not the sort of thing that could have prepared me in any way for what was to come.

At any rate here, in full is what I came to remember as I stretched out indolently and gazed at the spray on the arched body of that stranger, or what I remembered later that day and night, or what I thought I remembered, about that place. The place was what I saw the most clearly, so I might just as well begin there.

The walls of the house were covered over with some sort of thick creeper that very possibly hid rats amongst its trumpet-shaped orange flowers. For some reason I remember someone mentioning rats in connection with that creeper. It may have been an aunt who touched on the matter of the presence, or what she feared was the presence, of some kind of rodent in that creeper.

The furniture was what one would expect in that sort of a place, dreadfully heavy and somber and almost without any sort of distinction at all. There was a dark green billiard table that matched the dark purple curtains and the dark mahogany of the dining room table. And all the time, though the sea was not actually visible from the house because of the unusually thick vegetation, the air was full of its harsh presence. One could hear the constant pounding of the surf, as the huge waves broke on the sand.

Don't you remember her house, an old turreted building with a corrugated iron roof and birds nesting in the roof? Afterward the house became a home for the mentally retarded. The aunts moved out; no one wanted it.

. . .

"I remember nothing of hers, nothing at all," I suppose I said indifferently.

I do remember, you know, some of the names of the girls at school. Not many. I remember something about the body of a girl, perhaps the broad shoulders of a girl. What was the name of that broad-shouldered girl on the swimming team who had climbed into bed one night with another girl and played the lover? Was it Rathbone or Hadfield or Radcliffe, something like that? It has no importance, of course. Or I remember the wave of a hand from a window, but not the name of the girl who waved.

For some reason I remember a particularly hideous clock, which was proudly displayed, one of those horribly hybrid objects that does not belong to any particular period or place, where one finds certain echoes from the eighteenth century in its curves, but where the wood and the gloss of the gold is obviously from a later date, one of those pathetic objects whose mute ugliness has a certain quality one might almost call pathos and compare to the face of an idiot or of an abused child. I suppose the thing must have stood in the hall—a grandfather clock, I imagine you would call it, a tall affair, topped with what appeared to be gold figurines: angels or mythological figures, perhaps carrying torches or candles or trumpets. It may have been an aunt of this girl's who mentioned to me, with proprietary pride, that this ridiculous affair was wound once a week by a man who came expressly for that purpose.

The whole place was not only silent, apart from the sound of the surf, but was kept as dark as possible, which was probably just as well. Perhaps these static, tomblike rooms came to me this way because my memory of the place was literally dim, like those shadowed dreams that come to us half-lit. I saw these rooms darkened by time, or perhaps quite simply by facing south, or perhaps the curtains and shutters were kept closed to keep the rooms cool or to preserve the colors of the fabrics that were, nevertheless, sufficiently turbid. Whoever was responsible for the decorating of that place—I presume it was the aunt or the aunts, or the ancestors of the aunts—was evidently rather partial to mauve. Everything—at least as I remembered it—was in shades of mauve, running from pale lilac to puce.

Though, of course, I did not realize it at the time, it was in this house that the Summers girl waited for me that day, and from this house that she left the night she died, gliding down the steps at dusk, or so I was told, and going through the white gates of the garden only minutes before her body was lost.

Come to think of it, I believe I was mistaken as far as that island is concerned. I do not think that pink beach is on Mortorio at all, but on another of the small islands. There are so many of them, you know, and they all look more or less alike; it is hard to keep them straight. Wherever it is, the pink beach, it turned out, was no longer pink at all, if it had ever been that color, was not even pale pink, but actually a rather disappointing white, tinged at the edges with a thin line of pink. The water, I must admit, was quite exceptionally clear and cool. I lay on the cushions, gazing down at the sea for a while, before I let the German fellow coax me in once again, and we swam together a little way from the boat onto the shore. The fellow reclined in the sun at my feet, while I propped myself up against a tree in the shade and observed the light on the water. The wind had died down to a soft, warm breeze and the sea was perfectly still except for a faint rippling on the surface of the water and the almost imperceptible sigh of a small wave as it gathered and broke on the white sand.

Though the sun was no longer at its height, its light slanting obliquely, the rays were still warm. They caught the edge of an occasional cloud, and for a moment a shadow passed over the small strip of sand and across the water. There was no one on the beach except the two of us. The skipper had remained on the boat, where, I suppose, he polished off a bottle of chianti and promptly fell asleep in the sun.

Though I gathered from certain unmistakable signs that the German fellow would rather have liked to undress me—or rather to remove the black string, which would, after all, not have been too difficult a feat—and to go about his business, he apparently thought that any such action would be inappropriate just then. I shall not bore you with a detailed account of these proceedings, as they did not, at this point anyway, go very far. Besides, I am not, naturally, concerned with sex—anyone can fill in the necessary details of animality. Suffice it to say that I dallied with the man for a while or anyway allowed him to continue to where he imagined it was necessary to talk of, or actually confused what it was he was feeling with, love.

I have no idea what he said except that it was rather long and apparently detailed, and that the word love recurred often, and that he punctuated what he said with the question, "What are you thinking?" to which I replied, "Nothing," or "My mind just drifted."

"That's not possible," he said and told me how mysterious and forbidding he found my silence.

What I was thinking of, to tell you the truth, was not of love. I do not know and have never cared to know much about love, but of desire. I was thinking of the first time I remember feeling desire.

It was at school at the grave of the High Commissioner, which still remained in the grounds, on the flank of what was called a *koppie*. The place was considered out of bounds. We were not allowed to go there except on accompanied walks—"You never know, some native might be lurking!"—that were carried out in double file in our short green tunics, worn four inches above the knee, measured kneeling, and heavy, lace-up shoes, under the void of the sky and the harsh glare of the sun, across the flat veld, behind the gym teacher, marching through long grass and singing "Onward Christian Soldiers" loudly.

The site of the grave was a strange, solitary place with that mysterious stillness that comes with the sun and the heat. The tombstone, surrounded by eucalyptus and great, gray boulders, was a large, flat, mottled, gray-white slab of marble with a faded inscription in gold letters commemorating the man, the High Commissioner, a particularly gallant servant of Her Majesty the Queen and the British Empire, we were told, who had valiantly carried the flag and the hopes and illusions of England to this wild place, leaving far behind his beloved green hills and the misty isle. Beside the High Commissioner's grave was the smaller, gray slab of the same mottled marble, commemorating the death of the High Commissioner's dog.

Sometimes, someone, one girl or the other—there

were only girls in that place, would accompany me to the grave, to watch the sunsets, those extraordinary southern sunsets, when the sky was lit up a lambent gold, slipping surreptitiously across the veld at dusk and lying beside me on the tombstone.

What I remembered, while the wind began to pick up and the waves gathered and broke with a sigh on the shore, was one particular evening, when the girl I was with scattered wild poppies across the grave, orange poppies, with bright, loose petals like crepe paper, which, once uprooted, died fast. She lay there amongst the dying poppies, stretched out across the cool marble, looking up at the empty blue sky. A faint breeze fanned her cheek and lifted the hem of her green tunic.

There was something about the way she scattered poppies on the tombstone and then lay there herself, something light and quick, and at the same time reckless, something that one might even call abandonment, something that might be said to approach the poetic, about laying bright orange poppies with petals like crepe paper on a grave.

Somehow the orange of those poppy petals and the site of the High Commissioner's grave were associated in my mind with what I am obliged to call lust. I was not really sure why, at that point. I was distracted by the soft sound of the waves and the drone of the German's voice. It was later, when the German had finally left me, that I came to remember what had occurred at the grave.

What is rather astonishing, I suppose, is that I did not see it for what it was. It happened almost every day. I am sure of that. I knew, of course, when it was coming on, from certain small signs that would probably not have been visible to anyone else—something about the lips, a certain folding about the mouth, like a flower twisting its petals closed on the night. But it came on really rather suddenly. At any given moment it could make its appearance. And then would follow the odd moods, the shifts and sudden anger, the buying of extravagant gifts or the midnight sorting of some musty closet, or sometimes nothing at all. But I was unable to find a name for it at the time. I was quite unable to find a name for Mother's malady.

I can speak of all of this now directly, or can speak, anyway, of as much as I care to, without any fear of indiscretion, as Mother, of course, is dead. Did I mention that she died quite a while ago? I am not sure exactly when. I have never attempted to discuss her before, naturally, not only because I felt no desire to speak of an existence that is really of little interest, but because her presence, however remote, obliged me to remain in the domain of shadow. I did not entirely understand her purpose, as a child, but I understood it better than she realized.

The German fellow, Hans or Jan or whatever his name was, crumpled the cellophane paper from a packet of cigarettes in his long fingers. I watched the paper glint in the bright light. He lit up a cigarette and offered me one, which I refused. I took advantage of this pause in his discourse to suggest we leave the beach. The wind was already strong by then. I feared a rough ride. The German finally tired of talking of love and took me back to my hotel.

It was a wild ride, the boat slapping against the swell of the waves, as they gathered, overbalanced, and fell. The sun was beginning to sink, and the water shot through with a soft pink and blue, but as the waves approached the shore they were devoid of light and fell in folds against the rocks.

The motion of the boat on the roiling sea left me slightly nauseated and shaky at the knees. I said good-bye to the German with something like relief. The chap was becoming tiresome. Despite my wide-brimmed straw hat and the suntan lotion I always applied, my skin felt burned. My shoulders were painful, and my throat and ears ached from the wind. Salt had dried on my skin, and my hair was full of sand. I left the German, who lingered on in the lounge of the hotel, playing the grand piano with more emotion than skill—Chopin, I imagine—while I went to my room to undress.

I did not remember exactly what the man in Gerzett had said, nor did I particularly care. I had no desire to think about the man.

As I unzipped my tapestry bag, where I keep my inhaler, and pumped, standing at the window, watching a sea gull swoop down over the water, I remembered the man's hands on my body as he spoke of the fly, the dryness of his hands, the darkness of the skin of his hands, the hair on the back of his hands, and the cleanliness of the nails, the sureness of the touch. He had very strong hands.

She was scooping at a spider with a piece of white paper. Though I could not see the girl's features or even exactly what she was wearing, I noticed how the stuff of her dress clung to the shape of her body, or rather was blown against her body. Not that I was particularly interested in the shape of her body, but from the vague contours of her body, from some plumpness or something unfinished about her figure, or perhaps from her movements, from something careless about the way she crouched on the floor, threw herself down, scooping at the spider and, at the same time, from something not a little awkward, self-conscious, I realized that this girl was very young. Perhaps it was the rounded arms, or the skin of the arms, honey-hued and slightly freckled, or just the wrists, the loose, lithe wrists, that gave me the impression that this Summers girl was probably sixteen or seventeen at the most, down on her hands and knees, saving the life of a spider.

I wondered then, vaguely, lighting up a cigarette, turning from the window, what I had been doing with this girl in that room. I wondered if the man in Gerzett had been correct, if his words had some validity after all.

I asked myself if I had made this girl's acquaintance at school. I had the impression that this was probably not the first time I had seen this girl. What I mean is, I realized I must have seen her before I saw her save the life of a button spider. I must have met her before, if she had telephoned me to beg me to come to her house. I thought that we had probably both just finished school, or we may have met during some holiday toward the end of our last year in that school that lay in the valley, where the air was always damp and warm, and a harsh wind blew from the sea with a hollow sound through the ragged leaves of the strelitzia trees.

It seemed to me then that while I was in the room with this Summers girl, at her place, where the bay windows opened onto the garden, we had talked, or rather she had talked. I had no idea what she was talking about, but I could not help but realize that she was not only brushing her hair but that she was also talking to me.

Though I was not particularly interested in this girl, or what she might have been saying, it did occur to me then, that her words might have had some sort of significance, if what the man on the terrace had said had any validity. If this girl was to die a few hours after talking to me, her words might have had some significance. Vaguely, I wondered what a girl like that would have been talking about under those circumstances, though I was not aware at the time of what the circumstances were.

Come to think of it, I am not quite certain of the circumstances of Mother's death, either; I was not there at the time.

I had already taken up residence in England, you know, and received the news rather late. Certain moments during that period of my life have remained with me. I was, at the time, engaged in what is usually called, I believe, a love affair, with a younger and rather indifferent man. As a matter of fact, to tell you the truth, I find I do have a penchant for younger men. They do not usually expect as much conversation, do they?

As for this one, I remember the sumptuous softness of the skin, the body. The body was actually a little on the thin side; he may even have suffered from some malady for all I know. I do not really remember. Nor do I remember the face well. I suppose I hardly looked at the face, but I do remember the delicacy of the touch. Of course, the whole affair did not last much longer than the man's indifference.

I had forgotten about the eyes, the man's eyes. It was the eyes, you know, that were dark, the eyes were an ordinary green-brown but turned dark, seemed to turn almost black at times. There was something both caressing and at the same time hard, almost ruthless, in the gaze of the man in Gerzett.

I remembered his telling me about his profession. It seemed to me then, with the wind howling, as I began to walk about the room undressing, removing my damp robe, my bathing suit, my sandals, that the man in Gerzett had said he had been a doctor of some sort, perhaps a medical doctor, perhaps even a surgeon. He might very well have been a surgeon, I decided, a man who spoke without elegance but with not a little education; and there was the touch, the strength of the hands. He probably told me that he had been a man of the medical profession but, apparently, had not practiced for many years. He, too, had been wandering for some time, I believe he said. I remembered his words almost exactly then, and as I remembered them that sound came to me anew, I actually thought I could hear the sound of his shoes squeaking. But what he said was quite reasonable from a medical point of view, from any point of view.

You never know whether to tell them they are going to die or not; either way you are in for it.

What I had forgotten was that while this girl, the Summers girl, was talking to me in the room with the bay window, the telephone must have rung. She must have answered the phone at some point, while I was watching the jacaranda blossoms fall or the light. Probably she just sat there, letting the phone ring and going on talking to me. Perhaps I was the one to suggest she answer her phone, the sound of the ringing distracting me.

She may have lifted the receiver with an impatient

movement, said something, and then covered the mouthpiece with one hand and asked me some question. Someone was asking her if he could call on her. Perhaps she held up the receiver and looked at me and hesitated.

I suppose I would have shrugged my shoulders. Undoubtedly, if she had asked my opinion, I would have considered that it came to the same thing whether he came or did not come.

Perhaps I even said, "Go ahead, why not let him come?"

I do not believe she remembered the man's name, some man whose acquaintance she had made the night before at a dance at her house.

There were receptions at night, at times, in the garden, between the time of Father's death and Mother's remarriage. A trestle table was covered with a starched white cloth and placed under the willow tree. I was given the hors d'oeuvres tray to pass around the lawn in the half-dark, strutting about in the damp grass in thin pink slippers and striking up interesting poses as I passed around the silver tray with the anchovy paste on tiny pieces of toast and small pearl onions precariously pronged between morsels of cheese and minuscule sausages. I carried the tray aloft. I do not remember the faces of those people, or what they talked about, but the whole affair seemed to me most excruciatingly long and tedious. Afterward, before retiring, I was sent around again to be kissed and received a damp kiss and a fondle from each more or less inebriated guest.

By then, too, it had generally happened to Mother. I noticed that her smile, which had glinted somewhat gaudily in the blue light, had slipped, that the lips had folded, the lipstick running in the fine lines around the lips, or her blue eyelids had drooped somewhat over her sultry eyes, or a lock from a chignon had strayed, or a silk stocking twisted around an ankle, so that the seam meandered up into the folds of her dress, or sometimes, her whole self simply slid down from her chair and lay sprawled heavily across the grass.

Even putting aside the question of her death, or her reported death, I asked myself what she could have been saying to me. Or rather, the question that occurred to me—as I knew nothing about this Summers girl—was: what did people out there generally talk about?

It seemed to me, as I walked about my room, unpinning my hair, removing my damp suit, and stepping into the shower, that, out there, they were almost always talking about the same topic of conversation, they were almost always talking about the servants.

There was no denying it, it was an almost constant topic of conversation. They did not talk much about the weather out there, the weather being generally glorious, but they talked endlessly of their servants, with what seemed to me to be an almost morbid fascination. They always said exactly the same things. They might say, "Give them an arm and they'll take a leg," or "Darling, it's not that they're lazy, but they have no idea of time." It was quite extraordinary how everyone used exactly the same words. It did not matter who was speaking. The same things were said again and again and listened to with the same interest over and over, like a child listening to the same fairy tale told in exactly the same words, insisting that it should be told with the same words.

There was a code, you could call it a code, I suppose, that people used when they were talking about their servants out there, in that particular place and at that particular time, though, I would venture to suggest, what I cannot, of course, verify, that people have always been talking about servants in just about the same way.

It was the most boring of subjects, I always thought, the subject of servants being second only to diets for the provoking of ennui, and I thought, as I turned my face up to the water in the shower, that if this Summers girl had spoken of the servants, which it seemed to me quite likely she did, I could hardly have been expected to listen, would probably not have listened anyway, even if I had not been distracted by the light and the falling blossoms. Perhaps this girl had spoken to me of one particular servant, I thought; if she had, it would have been very difficult for me to remember a particular servant in that house, the name of a particular servant.

The light was gold in the trees. I was certain of the quality of the light. What I remembered or rather saw clearly was the light, the quality of the light out there, in that place.

I was not so sure about the servants. As I stood under the shower, letting the water beat down hard on my skin, washing the sand from my skin and hair, it occurred to me that I might have been mistaken, that this girl might not have been talking about servants but, rather, might have spoken of something she remembered. She might have been asking me if I remembered something that had occurred at school. But there under the shower I was not sure what she had asked.

Besides, I was thinking about Mother's clothes, or rather the place where she kept her clothes. I was thinking of Mother's closets. As I stood under the shower in the hotel bathroom, my eyes closed, rinsing the sand from my hair, I was not thinking about this Summers girl, or the man I met on the terrace in Gerzett, but Mother's closets.

For some reason I remembered a secret place, hidden at the back of a closet in the under side of a drawer where Mother kept her jewelry. Mother would plunge her hand and forearm avidly into the depths of the drawer to feel for the exact spot that caused the drawer to spring open. It was an almost perfect hiding place. She would drag forth the Craven A tin where she concealed her precious things, wrenching off the lid with trembling fingers to grasp her many different-colored rings, the canary yellow diamond, the deep blue sapphire, the flawed emerald, the ruby, the garnet, and the aquamarine, with which she arrayed herself.

All of Mother's closets smelled of that musty perfume that led me to suspect that there lay, between the folds of her innumerable garments, some secret, buried object I had never been able to discover.

Sometimes I hid in the back of her closet to count the "*tickies*" which she kept concealed there in what I remember as a large whiskey bottle, but it may have been gin. As for the closet, it was a place where she could not find me. I would hear her calling, but I remained in the dark behind the perfumed clothes with the coins.

She was brushing her hair impatiently and trying to get me to remember something that had happened at school.

"Surely you couldn't have forgotten," she might have said.

The fish pond. I remembered something odd, something quite absurd, but at the same time dangerous, happening at school at the fish pond. I could see the place, the surface of the brown water all covered over with lily pads, the lacquered shine on the lily pads, the way the fish swam together and then, with a flick of their tails, apart, could hear the sound of the bullfrogs croaking and then of someone playing the gramophone. Actually, what I remembered most clearly was the quality of the light. It was the kind of light that does not seem to be reflected by the objects but rather glows from within. The petals of the orange and yellow cannas burned morbidly. A dappled stone wall, all overgrown with moss and flowers, arched above the fish pond. I was stretched out there on the moss-covered stone reading a book, when one of the girls startled me in some way.

But what had actually happened at the fish pond was not of great interest to me. I had begun to think of something else. For some reason I was thinking about that teacher at school, the maths teacher, a Miss B—I really cannot remember her name.

I am almost positive that Miss B, unlike Mother, who possessed a vast, padded, laced-and-boned collection of one-pieces and two-pieces with or without suspenders and bows, never wore that garment that Mother considered essential for a fully developed woman. Perhaps it was as a consequence of this lack of foundation that Miss B drooped and then fell from grace. She was actually banished from that place of learning. She was brought before Miss Spinny, the head mistress, who had a wart on her chin. Miss B was brought before Miss Spinny and Miss Spinny's pug dog, who snapped at Miss B's heels. Miss B lurched, stiff-legged, down the stone steps, with her cardboard suitcase swinging beside her, alone. Her downfall had something to do with an A on a maths test that should have been an F.

Figures, I'm afraid, were never my strong point.

Something odd had probably happened one day at the fish pond or at the grave of the High Commissioner or in the dormitory, and this girl, no doubt, was trying to get me to remember what it was, on the day I spent with her at her place. She was talking about a jump or perhaps the moonlight or even the sound of the cicadas or the smell of the eucalyptus trees. But I was studying the painting.

The little girl in the painting glowed morbidly. There was a painting hanging on the wall, perhaps over the bed in the room with the bay window, at this girl's place. I remembered the room with the bay window and a blackboard along one wall and over the bed, this painting.

It was a painting that had probably been hanging there for some time, might have been hung there and then forgotten, the kind of painting placed on the walls of children's rooms, the kind of pretty, sentimental painting that I have always found distasteful.

I do not think of childhood as a time of innocence, you know. I was certainly in no way an innocent child. I remember distinctly, long before I was ten, killing off all the girls in my class, one by one, in my mind, killing off the plainer, less interesting girls first and fast and lingering over the beauties, killing the beauties off slowly with exquisite and, for someone habitually devoid of imagination, rather inventive tortures which I accomplished with delectation.

. . .

The painting was probably some copy of a nineteenth-century painting, perhaps by a follower of Gainsborough or Reynolds, a painting of a little girl whose face is seen in profile, a face painted in an attempt to render what the artist must have conceived of as the innocence of a child or the spontaneity of a child or the eagerness of a child to step forth and engage in what is generally known as the fullness of life: rosy cheeks, soft blond curls, candid, wide-spaced blue eyes, a gently smiling mouth, tiny, pearly ear. The artist had done his work with some skill, a certain ability with paint, but for some reason the man had painted the little girl with her legs tucked up into the full skirt of her dress so that, when one first looked at the picture, it seemed that the little girl in the frothy yellow dress had no legs at all, that she would never be able to run forth and embrace anyone or anything and certainly not the fullness of life.

Or that is what I thought when I stared at that painting; I remember thinking that this child would never jump to what would undoubtedly have been delicate little feet and run to greet someone she loved: perhaps a father or a mother, uncle or aunt or a small brother or perhaps even a friend, that the child would remain seated there in her frothy yellow dress, waving her dimpled hands.

That was what I was thinking as I examined the painting, and this Summers girl was talking to me.

I wondered if the legs of the child in the painting were actually visible or perhaps, though tucked up, suggested by a knee at the edge of the dress or even by the simple means of a pair of shoes which, undoubtedly, would have been dainty, perhaps even little brown slippers, which emerged from the edge of the dress.

Surely the painter had not forgotten the legs or the shoes?

Surely you must remember something about this girl: her house, her relatives, or even her servants? She did nothing but talk about you. I'm certain she spoke of you when you left the room. I'm sure she said you were at school together. She said you were her best friend. Or that she had met you as a small child. Perhaps you were thrown together by your nannies? Was that it? Or were you actually cousins or some sort of distant relations? She kept talking about you. She said how much she admired you, how clever you were, how courageous or independent. She said something like that. She went on and on.

Surely you must remember some feeling you had for her?

I must have answered that I was not in the habit of noting and still less of remembering my feelings. It was probable that, had I known this girl, I would not have particularly disliked her. It is rare that I actually dislike anyone, though, who knows, I may have told the man that I might have wished her dead at some moment. After all, most of us do at some time or the other contemplate the death of people we know.

I was not at my home in the Cotswolds the night they called me. I was with the young man I think I mentioned. It was one of those nights of which I remember nothing—or nothing after that scent of warm flesh and the way the man's eyelashes swept down on his cheeks ardently. The maid received the news that she reported to me the next morning, swabbing at her eyes pleasurably and undoubtedly already counting the recompense this service might warrant and, what with her confusion and my own, and the time change, I was never quite sure when Mother died. What I remember is the rain. I was of course obliged to make that long trip out there.

It was after a period of drought that is so frequent in that country. During the funeral it began to rain. It rained for three days almost constantly, the rivers rising and breaking their banks, eroding the land, sweeping away the red topsoil, rushing down to the sea. The rain beat down on the earth brutally, stopping for only a moment with a weak glimmer of sunlight piercing the thick clouds. I remember, first, the sudden sound of the rain on the corrugated iron roof of the church. The first hard, sparse drops beat down on the roof of the church and the dry earth, interrupting the droning of the priest's voice. The rain turned to hail almost immediately, the stones as big as bullets that burst as though loosed from a gun. They scattered down the stained-glass windows with a brutal clatter.

Afterward, we stood around outside the stone church for a moment under black umbrellas, the rain splashing the red mud of the church garden onto my stockings. I remember the broken red roses in the garden behind the church and the sound of the rain and the ominous rumble of the thunder which drowned out what the people were whispering to me as they leaned toward me to offer their condolences. All I perceived was the rain and the thunder and some other sound, perhaps the snuffling of some woman, or the keening of the black women who stood at the back of the church. Glistening black cars lined the street leading to the church. The windshield wipers started up as soon as we left the church, beating back and forth helplessly under the downpour.

It was a short, sudden downpour and then a pause filled with the rumbling of thunder and flashes of lightning and then the rain again, rain that turned fast to hail and was accompanied by forked lightning, alternating with sheet lightning, illuminating the sky.

Odd, isn't it, how literature can make one weep? I have wept copiously over the death scenes in Dickens, but I never shed a tear at Mother's funeral.

My thoughts were disturbed by a knock on the door. It was the German again. He had not gone back to his hotel, after all.

I will admit that he did appeal to me in some fashion. I will even confess, entre nous, that his body aroused me quite unusually. I am not absolutely certain what it was about the chap that appealed to me. Perhaps it was the long legs or the blond forelock or quite simply the outrageous flattery, the way he stared at me with something close to adoration in the candid blue eyes, or possibly it was because I had not engaged in this sort of activity since my illness in the mountains, or perhaps the memories that had assailed me continuously that day had aroused me in some strange way. At any rate, I made the mistake of letting the man enter my room before dinner, which is not my habit.

He made some jocular comment about always catching me emerging from water. I stood with my towel around me, the water trickling across the tiled floor, the room full of steam. The simplest thing to do was to allow him to enter and have him dry my back.

When that task had been accomplished thoroughly, I

let him lie beside me and touch my body. My mind continued to wander. As he caressed me, I was thinking of the man in Gerzett.

Although I never knew her well, hardly spent more than a couple of hours with her, when it was all over, I could see there was really no meanness in her, no showing off; she didn't seem to have learned how to protect herself at all. She was the sort of girl who would never have hurt anyone, not even a fly.

She was sitting on the stool before the dressing table and talking to me. I was watching her hair, though I could not really tell you the color of her hair—perhaps a nondescript brown—or even the color of her eyes. I was watching the brush she dragged fast through her hair and the breeze lifting the curtains and out there in the garden a blur of mauve and flame from the jacarandas and the flamboyants and from the spring green that was almost gold.

Through the half-opened curtains, I could see an alley of jacaranda trees, a whole double row of them, going from near the house across the garden down to the edge of the wild veld and bamboo shoots. The jacaranda trees were still in bloom, though the blossoms were beginning to fall, pale, mauve, fragile blossoms lifted up to the sky or floating down slowly to the ground below, caught in the breeze for a moment, before they fell to where they lay scattered between the trees in splashes of light and shade. What I could see from the bay window were the jacaranda trees and the blossoms that lay on the ground and the green lawns that ran back into wild veld that stretched out like a hand to the distant, gray-blue hills.

She was trying to get me to remember something or other. I was not sure why she had begged me to come and spend the day with her and then proceeded to force me to remember some event at school. I was vaguely aware that she was not getting to the heart of the matter. I was looking at the painting on the wall and watching the brush she was dragging through her hair and her narrow wrist. She had a loose, lithe wrist.

The brush was an ornate silver one, part of a set, the sort of beaten silver brush-and-comb set women owned in those days. Her initials, D curled into an S, may have been on the back of the brush.

The rest of the set, the comb and the mirror, I believe, lay on the dressing table before her, but she had the brush in her hand, and she was brushing with quick, impatient strokes, her hand clasped well up the handle of the brush in a way that was almost greedy, holding the brush tightly and dragging the brush again and again through her hair as though there were something she wished to take from her hair or her head by brushing her hair again and again.

The early morning was already warm and humid with that mysterious stillness that comes, it has always seemed to me, with the sun, as it comes with the snow, as though the sun brings a certain dead quiet.

A summer morning, I suppose it might have been a summer morning, or what is generally called summer, though, down there at this girl's place, being at a lower altitude, in the valley and near the sea, the seasons slip one into the other almost imperceptibly. Perhaps it was actually spring, the end of spring, as the last of the jacarandas were still blooming, and the flamboyants were already in flower. It could have been the end of October, what the people out there call *die mooiste maand*, the prettiest month—it was not April, not spring in April—but spring in October, with that sultry feeling in the air and yet, even in the early morning, the breeze stirring just the tips of the trees and the mauve jacaranda blossoms floating down slowly to the ground.

It was like a conversation overheard in a chamber with thin walls, sounds coming from next door, unintelligible sounds but still the tone of voice audible, tiresomely audible. It was like an interminable conversation that somehow penetrates through a wall and even into sleep.

There was something pleading in the tone, something harsh, dissonant, strident. There was something about the tone that was curiously raw, ugly, embarrassing, something almost degrading about the tone of voice. She was begging. She continued in this vein for quite a while, as far as I remembered, though at that point I was not remembering much.

The German was still beside me, having given up any pretense of drying my back or rubbing my skin with the soothing unguent I had handed him. I was naturally a little distracted by the stealthy movements which brought his heated body to press urgently up against mine. He was obviously in a state of arousal that could not easily be ignored. In an attempt to engage me more actively in his lovemaking, he had placed his swollen life in my hands, exhorting me to handle it with more enthusiasm than I had shown as yet. His moaning had begun to penetrate my consciousness.

There was something that seemed quite ridiculously exaggerated about what she said to me. It may have been, "Don't you see, you are the only one who can really help me," or

"I have to tell you, and only you, about this," or perhaps, "I know you'll understand."

I asked her, I presume, not to exaggerate, not to get carried away. I told her that she undoubtedly overestimated me, that there was probably not much I was able to do for her or for anyone, and continued to let my gaze wander around the room, watching the light that lay like a string of beads on the floor, watching the flutter of the net curtain in the bay window. I may have said I did not think there was much we could do for one another and made an attempt to speak of other matters.

Perhaps I asked her what she was going to wear to the school dance, or whom she was going to invite. The absurd thought that crossed my mind was, I remember this clearly, that she was collecting money, that she had been assigned to invite all the girls in the class to ask for money for the school. The old building was always in need of some repair or other.

But of course that was not what she had in mind. She had not adopted the tone of voice one adopts to collect money.

Perhaps I mentioned something about some young man. There were quite a few young men who visited me then, you know. As a matter of fact, I had made quite a large collection of young men and, I suspect, had already allowed a certain amount of fondling to take place on warm nights in the half-dark of certain gardens, wandering out of French doors across smooth lawns, climbing *koppies*, picking burrs from nylon stockings, sitting on rough branches, and letting hands wander freely.

My maidenhood, I presume, was still intact. No doubt, I had no intention of giving it up lightly. Still, I really could not tell you for certain if I still had it—as a matter of fact, I am not actually quite sure when I lost that prized article. The first time I remember engaging in what I believed to be the relinquishing of that jewel, there was absolutely no sign that I had relinquished anything at all, if you see what I mean. It was a singularly painless, unsullied moment of no consequence, one that led me to the definitive conclusion that I was not *intacta*. Perhaps the treasure I believed to have guarded so jealously had actually escaped unawares on some bicycle ride or a climb over some wall or perhaps even during some forgotten fumble.

Every evening she brought me to her bed, or perhaps I had been there all through the hot afternoon, napping. Every evening, in the time between Father's death and my stepfather's coming, I lay on the bed and watched, as Mother dressed for dinner.

All her movements seemed slow, languorous; Mother seemed almost motionless.

There was the blue light that filtered through the lined chintz curtains. There was the thick carpet with the pomegranate pattern that muffled her steps; the place was quiet.

Before she put on her apparel, in the early evenings, she sat sipping whiskey and soda on the bed in her silk gown, her face pale. "Would you like to bring me the other half," she said, stretching out her glass, the silk sleeve of her gown falling away from her forearm. The siphon was covered with what seemed to me a fine silver net. I pressed down carefully on the silver lever to eject a steady stream of bubbling water. I said, "Say when." The glass was cut with an ornate pattern. There was a stain of white powder and red lipstick on the rim. I carried the glass to her, walking slowly across the room with my eyes on the liquid in the glass. I handed it to her, not watching her but hearing her as she threw back her head and drank with thirsty gulps. She gave me a sip to drink from the bottom of the glass and asked me if I loved her.

"Give me a kiss," she said.

Through the lifted, cut-glass beaker I could see the white powder on the edge of the glass, the trace of the lipstick, and the blue light in the curtains. I could see the thick carpet and through the door the dressing room with the closets and the *tickie* bottle and at the end by the window the closet with the secret drawer.

Mother rose languidly from the bed, that slightly sour, mysterious odor of buried objects perfuming the air. In the half-light she stretched, standing before the window. The pale flesh glistened as she pulled the transparent haze of her gown over her head.

Mother's full form, half clothed and blanched, disturbed the dim light. Without her makeup her face was a mask with faint traces of lipstick in the lines around her mouth. Her eyelids sank heavily across her sultry eyes.

She unscrewed the top from a round, cut-glass bottle and leaned forward to pour the liquid into a cupped hand. She splashed the gold eau de cologne against her skin. The sweep of her body caught the light. She patted her throat and the damp curls that grew in mysterious places with a fluffy pink powder puff, the talcum powder falling around her toes like fine ashes.

At first I was not sure whether it happened before or after she had saved the spider, or even before or after she told me about the dream. I supposed that she must have moved from where she sat by the dressing table, brushing her hair, and come over toward me.

I thought it was while I was attempting to change the subject again by speaking this time of some ailment, of a headache or some other complaint. My illness, though it had not yet announced itself as such, was to declare itself in its true form shortly thereafter. It caused me, often enough, to avoid certain activities that made me breathless. I was never able to play any of the games that required the ability to run or jump and were considered so essential to the avoidance of any undesirable animal urges, and to the formation of character and other sterling qualities in young men and women out there in that place. I suffered, even then, from a dry cough, an aggravating, constant tickle in the throat, that kept me awake at night and responded in no way to any of the medicines prescribed and that no one was able to diagnose.

I thought it might have been as I spoke of my illness that she came over toward me to offer me her sympathy in some concrete form, but it may have been as she spoke of a dream.

There was a child drowning in the dream, and there was someone else in the dream, but, as I was not listening, I was not sure who the other person might have been. As I lay there on my rumpled damp bed with the German beside me, or rather the German leaning over me, his hands caressing my body, I tried vaguely to remember the people in this girl's dream, but I did not remember this Summers girl's words.

As a matter of fact, there are very few of Mother's words that I remember. I really cannot tell you much of what

Mother would say to me, only a few nursery rhymes, perhaps "Ride a cock horse to Banbury Cross" and "Little Miss Muffet," things of that sort. It is really the clothes I remember, even the sounds of the clothes: the snap of the half-petticoat over the bones of the corset, the sigh of the stockings rubbing together as she walked, and the suck of the damp heel against the leather of her loose sandal.

I think she said, "Listen to me please, just this once. I dreamed I was a child. I was sinking down through the water, and you dived down to bring me to the surface, but you couldn't find me in the water. You couldn't hear me calling to you."

She may have said, "Do you think it is bad luck to dream of a child?"

I probably said, "Don't be so absurd," or "Don't be such an idiot."

It was then that she spotted the spider, I think, and bent down, squatted on her haunches at first, and then actually got down onto her hands and knees and scooped at a small spider, a button spider, a tiny black spider, pushing a stiff piece of white paper against the carpet, chasing the spider with a piece of white paper, chasing it along the edge of the mauve carpet onto the parquet floor, again and again, turning the paper as it ran one way and then the other, until she caught it on the edge of the paper and ran to the window to set it free.

What I remembered then began only as this girl reached out to me, and when I knew she was afraid. It lasted from when she got up to come over to me until they called us to lunch.

From the start, of course, I was aware that she was afraid, but as she reached out to put her hand on my hand, I also knew that the thing was not done, had just begun. Someone was calling us for lunch, and I knew then that something was about to occur. I can only surmise that this Summers girl knew for some while that something was to occur, but I think I began to have an inkling of what was to occur right then, as I removed my hand from hers, as they called us for lunch. Perhaps it was just one of those impressions, you know, that come to us from time to time, the impression of returning to a situation that has already been resolved. Not that I was sure then how the situation would be resolved.

I was not sure then why this girl had her hand on my hand, but surely I should get to the point without any further preliminaries. This was how it happened that I banished the German from my chamber without his ever tasting of the fruit he had praised so extravagantly and then found myself assaulted with memories.

Just before the poor fellow was about to enter my body, raised up on his hands—he was not an inventive lover, his broad sunburned chest and shoulders and his large member looming over me, I was suddenly overcome by the peculiar but distinct impression that it was no longer this man—Hans or Jan or whatever he was called—who was leaning over me. In the dim light that filtered through closed shutters, with my eyes half shut and perspiration misting my view, the absurd but terrifying impression that came to me was that the long-legged German had been transformed into the man I had met on the terrace in the mountains, who loomed above me, his hirsute chest hanging over me. I was then overcome by such a sudden and strong fear of suffocation that I pushed him from my body roughly and told him to leave.

"I can't, I'm sorry, but I can't," was all the explanation I felt necessary to give the fellow, who lay doubled up beside me as though I had struck him. When he pleaded with me to be allowed to remain—he was not a little uncomfortable, you can imagine, I refused adamantly. Eventually he rose, pulled on his clothes, took one quick, wild look around the room, and, spotting my cut-glass bowl, the one Mother left me, picked it up and flung it down onto the tiled floor with what I can only call fury. The bowl shattered into a thousand pieces; the jewelry scattered across the floor. He left my room, slamming the door behind him and shouting something that was undoubtedly rather dreadfully rude but that escaped me as, fortunately, I do not speak German nor ever cared to learn that tongue.

But even once the German had gone, and I had called the maid to pick up the jewelry and the innumerable pieces of broken glass, the room seemed strange to me, unfamiliar, and I continued to hear the shiver of glass. The shadows on the rough, whitewashed walls looked ominous, and the doors to the bathroom and closet shut on secrets I felt it unnecessary to attend.

I opened the shutters on the evening light. It was that indeterminate moment of hesitation between day and the fall of night. The sky was still blue, but the land had caught the shadow, and the sea looked almost dark. Dark shadows blackened the water, and the lights of the harbor were lit and shimmered on the surface of the sea like oil. All the substance began to run from the colors; finally, only the black of the shadows and the white of the lights remained.

Walking restlessly about my room, avoiding the places where the faint light expired, touching my things, adjusting the place of an ashtray or the folds of the mohair rug on the end of my bed, I attempted to quiet my nerves. I felt curiously restless. I might even go as far as saying I felt perturbed. At moments I reached for my inhaler and pumped and even shuddered slightly thinking of the shattering of Mother's glass bowl.

The effect of these tiresome thoughts seemed to me out of all proportion to their appearance, but there was no point in denying it; my mind reverted constantly to the man's words, and his words brought with them memories I had thought were long since forgotten. The more I considered the matter, the more half-forgotten details I recollected. Like a prisoner in a cell, remembering his chamber at home, I could perceive, dimly at first, and then increasingly clearly, detail after detail. There seemed to be no end to them. I began to picture each object in that place with almost magnifying clarity: the curve of the balustrade on the staircase, the lacquer of the Steinway piano in what was called the lounge, the brass-studded kist in the entrance hall, the fat hydrangea tubs by the stable door, one pink, one blue.

What would ensue from this process of recollection I was, as yet, not a little uncertain; but I was aware, you know, even then, that my settled existence was in danger of being disturbed. I had no wish to disturb my settled existence. I have always been apprehensive of change; this apprehension is as familiar to me as the sound of the wind; I had no wish to commence anything anew.

I closed the shutters again on the evening light, lit up

the lamps, and sat in the arm chair, working on the petit point cushion I was embroidering and then letting my work fall from my hands, sitting gazing at the photograph of Mother in its silver frame, studying the slight tilt of the head, the length of the string of pearls, the line of the long-waisted dress.

I wished only to terminate that sense of seeing too much, of hearing too much, reviewing a past that was of no interest to me. I desired not much more than forgetfulness. I wished only to regain my usual complacency. However, at that moment, with the stillness of the night broken only by the sighing of the wind, a host of memories, as innumerable and as disparate as the pieces of my shattered glass bowl, continued to assail me.

I spent the rest of the evening and that night in my chamber. I did not go out for dinner. I even relinquished my nightly stroll and ice—I have an inordinate fondness for Italian ice cream. I did not feel the necessity to partake of anything at all then. I drew the heavy linen curtains tightly shut, showered again, and climbed into bed. I took half a sleeping tablet with a glass of mineral water—one cannot drink the water on that island, you know—and lay in that bed, naked under only a sheet, without any headboard, propped up high on white pillows, staring at the ceiling, struggling to breathe, listening to the sound of the wind, and thinking of the sea that was receding and then swelling forward perpetually.

What has always interested me has been the details, you know, just the details, those fragmentary instants that make up the stuff of our existence: the slant of a shadow on the sand, or the glow of a lamp on polished wood in the quiet of the evening, an ant with a crumb as it climbs under a log. I have spent hours watching ants climbing under logs.

So that what I remembered about that luncheon in that place—there was a meal, I realized, that day at that place—was the servant and particularly the sound of the manservant.

In that place, this Summers girl's place, I seemed to remember, lying in that bed, listening to the sound of the wind, they were all menservants, or the ones I had seen were menservants. They wore those uniforms that made them look almost identical, as schoolchildren look identical.

The uniform this one wore for serving at table was a white jacket and trousers, starched to a crisp, and worn with a broad red band that went over one shoulder and across the chest. What I remembered about this servant was not so much the band across his chest as the rustle of his starched uniform, just the rustle of the white starched uniform as the servant bent across the table, and the tassel. I particularly remembered the ridiculous tassel that swayed back and forth on the end of the broad red band, which lay across the servant's chest like some sort of decoration for an act of valor.

The servant tapped the bottle opener against a bottle of wine inquiringly, but no one seemed to notice. Above us a fan turned uselessly, stirring up the hot air, the blades whipping around unsteadily. The servant's uniform rustled while this Summers girl leaned forward to whisper something to me across the table, sotto voce, but I could not hear what she was saying through the delphinium. The pale blue petals of the delphinium fell onto the polished mahogany like shadows; the silver water pitcher misted over, pearls of moisture glistening on the rim.

. . .

All my life people have ignored me. I've got used to it. It's as though they look right through me. But it was different with this girl. She wasn't like the others.

The man on the terrace was attempting to tell me something about being ignored. He had had the feeling that people did not really notice him—his father, for one.

He was born, I suppose, in some small "*dorp*" in the Free State in a house that probably smelled of Jeyes fluid and pumpkin fritters, a house with a dry, dusty garden where strangled zinnias grew by the gate. It was probably one of those poor houses where polish takes the place of wealth, and cleanliness of style. I do not know, of course, if it was actually in a house of this sort that the man grew up, but I do remember that the man on the terrace in Gerzett said something about a father who had beaten him, or perhaps it was that the father had disappeared or done some other rather disreputable thing. There was definitely something peculiar about the father. Probably it was the father who had some kind of hallucinations, though it may have been the man himself who thought he could see lions standing on the tops of armoires, though that seems hardly likely. When he attempted to converse with his father, what his father was doing was staring at lions that stood on the tops of armoires.

They say, you know, that there is a great deal of mental illness amongst those people, that they have been away from civilization of any kind for so long on those vast, dreary farms, breeding among themselves often quite incestuously.

A railway man, I think he said the father had been,

something on the railways. Probably he had the sort of position the government found for those of their kind, whatever their education, because of their white skin.

Anyway, whatever the father was, the man in Gerzett was probably used to being ignored. He had probably been ignored by everyone and particularly by the English out there. The moment he opened his mouth, he must have seen that supercilious look in their eyes. He must have known they were wondering if he had hair on his back, beat the natives with a *sjambok* in his cups, or had engaged in some dark business with mother, sister, or brother.

It came upon her at the end of every afternoon in that hour when the sky was still lit up a translucent blue, but the room had turned dark. It happened so mysteriously that, like the fall of night, I could never tell, however hard I tried to catch the moment, just when it took her. She began to move slowly. I could hardly tell in that blue light whether she was moving or not.

Before Mother continued her evening toilet, I remember, just as I tell you this, how she would sit silently, motionless, on the edge of the mattress in her short shift, the bed giving slightly beneath her weight. But the moment I always watched carefully was the taking off of the most important of her garments, the foundation of Mother's rectitude.

It was the foundation garment that interested me.

The article was a most intricate, strapless garment, made of cream lace, whalebone, and white elastic. It was padded for extra fullness at the bodice and tapered mercilessly at the waist, conceded a little territory at the hips, and ended coquettishly and with a certain fantasy in the elastic suspenders that were studded all along the leg with small blue stars.

Before Mother removed this article, she sat slumped on the bed for a moment and held onto the thing, folding her arms along the whalebone against her chest, as though contemplating the task before her.

Then she began to wrestle with the thing.

First, she dragged it down a little way over her hips, starting off very slowly, swinging her hips slightly from side to side, easing the lace and bone across her thighs. She pulled, she sighed, she pushed, she breathed in short, thick pants, she grunted, she swore, she stopped to catch her breath and pour herself a glass of soda water from the soda siphon. Then, when she finally had the thing almost all the way to her knees, so that the dark secret shadow appeared again between the tops of her thighs, she struggled relentlessly anew to bring the thing up over the swell of her hips, as though she had changed her mind, was moved by some hope, buoyed up for a moment before the final fall. At last, she removed the article completely, and her flesh sagged about her, as though it were not part of her at all but some useless covering she would gladly have shed.

I tried to find something suitable to read. I was reading a book by an obscure French poet of the wrong century, but the words came to me distorted, laden with meaning; they sounded bizarre, took on new and sinister connotations. Certain words sparked off curious associations, and I kept reading the word *main*, which the poet was wont to use frequently, as *mort*, or suddenly saw it as the English word *man*, which brought my lecture to a halt with sudden incomprehension.

Despite myself I was thinking of this girl the man on the terrace had been going on about, or rather not thinking about this Summers girl but actually seeing her, seeing her quite clearly, my mind running on in a most tiresome way, so that the sensation of ennui became almost a physical one. It was difficult for me to think of the man's words without evoking this Summers girl and vice versa. It was as though they were one flesh, bonded in some way.

But not Daisy. Daisy didn't ignore me. She turned her head to me. She looked at me. She listened to me. She wanted to enjoy me, that's all. Or that's what I thought when I met her at that dance at her house, when she turned to me. When I came in the door, she was standing by the window, on the edge of her own party. She was just standing there. The sun was shining. I walked across the lawn and looked at those willow trees, hanging down like nets. When I went inside, she was standing there by the window, her skin all lit up. Her skin looked as transparent as the glass behind her.

Possibly the man said something jejune about seeing this girl for the first time at a dance at her place.

Probably what he had actually thought, when he first saw this girl, wherever he first saw her, was: One of those English girls, one of those rich, spoiled English girls who flirt with you and then hold back, do not give forth what has been promised; I'm going to make sure I get what I want from this one. But it is hardly likely the man would have told me something like that.

Although I didn't know her well, hardly spent more than a couple of hours with her, when it was all over, I could see there was really no malice in her. There was no meanness, no showing off. She didn't seem to have learned how to protect herself at all. She was the sort of girl who would never have hurt anyone, she was the sort of girl who would never have hurt a fly.

We ate, I believe, potted shrimp and some kind of salad, quite possibly potato salad, a little heavy on the mayonnaise, I suspect, followed by a trifle topped with whipped cream and nuts. We drank, I suppose, the servant obligingly filling our glasses as soon as they were empty.

The light on the veranda glinted on the glass. The fan whirred, the blades whipping unsteadily above us, stirring up the hot air.

I did not remember the conversation at first. I did not suppose there was much conversation. It was probably too hot, I thought, for any conversation at all. Besides, by the time the coffee arrived, I presumed I was feeling not a little exhausted and was quite possibly not listening to any conversation there might have been. My head was probably beginning to ache.

The heat seemed to increase with the progress of the meal.

The servant's starched uniform rustled, and he tapped the bottle opener inquiringly against the bottle of wine.

This Summers girl was whispering something through the delphinium, something about the bamboo shoots at the bottom of the garden. She was leaning across the table and whispering something about the bamboo.

The walls of the room were a stippled off-white that pleased me. The Italians, I will say, have taste, and the decor of those hotel rooms on the island was quite satisfactory. I have always liked white walls, white china, and come to think of it, many of my dresses are white, you know. White or black. The reason is, I suspect, that I am slightly color-blind; I do not quite distinguish certain colors, though they have always been important to me.

I remember the first time I saw snow. I must have been seventeen or eighteen, on my first visit to Europe. Mother took me skiing in Austria, I believe, with the intention of marrying me off to a lord. But what interested me was the snow. I did not even know that the stuff melted. I imagined it was like the cotton wool they used to decorate the Christmas trees out there. It was the whiteness of it that delighted me. I remember turning on my heels, spinning around in the stuff, feeling it fall wet and soft on my face.

I counted three tiny cracks in the white plaster on the ceiling of the hotel room. I lay on the bed, counting. I have a rather odd habit of counting, for someone who has never had much truck with figures. I add up numbers on license plates or count out the number of bars on windows or railings on a banister. In that room where I lay there were exactly seventy-seven reddish-brown, rather slippery tiles on the floor.

Though I had not been aware of this at the time, thinking back on it, I sensed that the man in Gerzett had been desirous of finding some sort of explanation, for what had happened. Not that I had asked for or even seen the need for anything approaching an explanation, or even thought such an explanation possible.

I wanted nothing to do with this man. I had certainly not questioned him in any way. But it seemed that he felt the need to explain what had happened the night this girl had died.

Why, why, why should something like that happen to her, of all people? There was something very gentle about her, very soft. I remember the way her hair curled around her face. Don't you remember the flush in her cheeks, and the way she blinked and then caught at her long eyelashes and held them between finger and thumb? At first, I thought it was an affectation, the blinking and the fingering of the long eyelashes. Then I realized she was shy. She was just shy with a stranger.

I remember the slight dampness of her touch.

There has to be some explanation for it all. I'm sure that if you would help me, if you would only talk to me for a minute, I might understand. You must remember something, after all, hey?

I said, most probably, that I was not in the habit of talking much, that there did not seem much to say, that quite possibly there was some quite simple explanation for it all, that he was wrong to insist on the matter, which was probably one of minor importance.

But the creature seemed to consider it was all of the utmost importance. He seemed to feel almost as though his own life depended on finding a meaning for the loss of this girl's. Personally, I could not see what the one had to do with the other. I was of the opinion that the loss of this girl's life had nothing to do with anyone else's.

I suppose I said I had difficulty remembering, that what I remembered most was probably the weather.

Because of my illness, I am one of those people who

are particularly sensitive to changes in the weather. I have to be very careful about drafts, and humidity is particularly noxious to my constitution. I do not do well in extreme heat, either. I try to keep covered in the sun. You know, I think a hat is most important. I really do not think women realize quite how important covering the head is for both the hair and the skin. And I find that, generally speaking, I am very easily fatigued and quite as rapidly bored. Life, it often seems to me, is made up of a series of rather boring pursuits. Take, for example, cutting one's toenails: what could be more boring than that!

What I remember, or what I notice, you know, more than anything else, is probably the light and the shadow. There is a certain moment when the leaves of the oak are alight, turned to transparent gold, that gives me a sensation quite close to and sometimes far superior to that which I believe is enjoyed in the act of lovemaking. I notice the sky particularly. For example, at Mother's funeral, as I said before, I remember only that the sky was a heavy steel gray and that it rained hard, the kind of rain that turns to hail out there. I remember the rain and the way the forked lightning lit up the sky, not much more than that.

The man on the terrace in the mountains kept asking why, why, why, as though there might be some sort of explanation, though at the time I had no idea what he felt it was necessary to explain. It had been too dreary, too dull, too melodramatic to interest me. I suppose I ended up by pretending to agree with the man, which is sometimes the only way to rid oneself of these people.

I really had not listened to all of that. I can only compare the sound of his voice to the dripping of a tap.

. . .

The soft white folds of her heavy flesh disturbed and disgusted me.

I could not remember what this girl was muttering at me through the delphinium, but I did, then, remember that someone else had said something during that luncheon, something quite extraneous, absurd. Someone muttered something in a rather grim, quiet voice. At first, I was not quite sure who it was that spoke, but it might have been an aunt. I remembered an aunt and then, as in a drunkard's vision, the aunt began to double, and I saw two aunts and then three. Could there have been three rather elderly, faded, prim women who blended into the gray of my forgetfulness? Or was this recollection something I had read of in some book or perhaps dreamed of in some dream?

I could see the three slightly ridiculous women vaguely, dressed in varying shades of mauve with prim, silver hair scraped back from their powdered foreheads, leaning across the table and murmuring together, like three minor characters from some Shakespeare play. "She was suffocated, you know," they said, speaking together, saying the identical thing, and I was sure that their names began with the same letter.

Not that I remembered or cared what the letter was, but I was almost certain the three women had never married, had remained maidens, though of course there was no way I could have known that, except by their odor, something musty mixed with lavender.

I saw the three women leaning over the luncheon table and dabbing at their foreheads with lace handkerchiefs. We had eaten lunch on willow pattern plates on the enclosed veranda. The servant served us lunch while the aunts sat upright, their white, spotted hands trembling slightly and almost invisible, like moths in the bright light, hovering over the plate of peeled shrimp and potato salad. They mumbled and muttered mysteriously.

For some reason I have the impression the aunts were speaking of some dreadful thing that had happened to a woman called Lola. An unspeakable thing had happened, they said. It was as we all sat in the trapped heat of the glassed veranda, and the blades of the fan whipped unsteadily above us, and the servant's starched uniform rustled, that the aunts muttered of the dreadful thing that had happened at twilight out on some stretch of barren veld.

The woman's name was Lola; for some reason I remembered the woman's name. I saw the woman with blond curls, stretched out in a short pink petticoat, her bare legs in the long grass. What I eventually deduced, after many circumlocutions and much shaking of the silver hair and fluttering of the hands, was that the woman called Lola had been assaulted, not only assaulted but murdered. She had been suffocated during the assault. We were left to imagine how this could have happened, or how the aunts said it had happened.

Three maiden aunts, who had lingered on for some reason in those still, moribund rooms with that dark and gloomy furniture, hovered around me when I arrived, greeted me on the doorstep or perhaps in the hall.

It was not only in fantasy that I was cruel as a child. There were actual moments. There was the time I forced some frightened new girl to eat the bitter juice of the aloe leaf, or the one when I taunted the girl fresh from England with the heinous crime of killing Joan of Arc. There was the rosy-cheeked boy who begged me not to call him Sticking-out-ears, and the girl called Landsberger whom I insisted on calling Hamburger.

You can't just forget a girl like that. She made an impression on you. She was something quite different. There was something about her. She had something soft, hesitant, a little tremble to the chin and at the same time an assurance, a kind of optimism, a kind of hope. It was difficult to put your finger on just what it was. Perhaps it was something she lacked. Something other people know instinctively or learn. Or perhaps, rather, it was something she had that no one else did. Not that she was a beauty, really. Surely you must remember something about her? A fairly big girl, tall, you know, quite tall, almost as tall as you are, a little on the plump side. It was only her coloring that made her pretty, that flush that rose from the neck like a promise. If she had had any luck, who knows what she might have done, hey? She might have gone from strength to strength, hey?

There was something lively about her, something shiny. She had an appetite for life. She kept blinking those big blue eyes at you, as though life was a bright affair. Don't you remember the way she blinked, her eyes filling with tears too easily? It seems to me her eyes were always filling with tears. I suppose you could say she was too easily moved. One violin in the background was enough to get her going. God, she had a glow to her skin, a flush in her cheek, a brightness in her eye. Don't you remember that, hey?

There was something enthusiastic, reckless, a sort of abandon in the way she moved, the way she spoke. She seemed graceful, though at times you might have said she was almost clumsy, awkward. She had that rare quality of seeming quite sincere, without even any awareness of snobbery. In a way, though she may have been suspicious of people, even afraid, she took everything at face value.

She had a kind of innocence, she more or less opened her heart up to you, to anyone, without reserve. That was part of the problem, I suppose. She probably opened her heart up to too many people.

She seemed very free in a certain way, as though she had not grasped life's limits.

Though I did not believe all of what the man told me, it is possible that in this instance he was at least partly accurate.

After all, in that town the girls, I suppose you could say, were different. Many of the girls of that town grew up continuously barefooted, half-naked, in all that sunshine, in all that space and fresh air, in the luxuriance of the land. Many of the young people out there had an insouciance, a lack of thought for the morrow, what one might call a looseness of limb, a frankness in the smile. It was a place, I suppose, free from the constraints imposed on young girls elsewhere.

Not that I was ever free. I liked rules and regulations, I liked a certain structure to my days, I liked the well-defined and the well-ordered. I did not like surprises. I had no time for the unforeseen or the extraordinary. I was not interested in anyone who was very different from myself; perhaps ultimately I was not really interested in anyone but myself, though there were, I suppose, moments when I watched others move.

. . .

The lily pads shone as though lacquered. Someone leaned over languorously to place the needle on the record, and one could hear the singing, as it rose and fell throughout the school garden.

It was very hot at the fish pond, though that did not seem sufficient explanation for what happened that afternoon. Actually, I could see no explanation for what happened that afternoon, but I remembered it as being a glittering afternoon, the school garden shining, the sun turning the leaves to small blades of light, the silver leaves that stirred and rustled in the faintest breeze, the shadows sunk to small deep pools at the roots of the trees. The garden was all light and abundance, and even the shortened shade seemed generous, a dark, cool, purple green.

Some girl, perhaps it was this Summers girl, I suppose, on due reflection, it might very well have been she, suddenly ran wildly across the lawn with her green tunic tucked up into her green knickers.

We wore straight green tunics and knickers with elastic around the leg that left a mark like a wound on the top of the thigh. Some girl, perhaps it was this Daisy, some girl with short blond curls and a certain glow to her skin had suddenly come running barefooted across the thick kikuyu grass.

I can still see the way she rushed suddenly across the lawn: it was the sort of exploit that might have been carried out to attract attention, I suppose, carried out so that every girl on the lawn would look up and watch, though in this case I am not certain it had been brought off with that purpose in mind.

Everyone looked up and watched.

Even I looked up and watched.

I was reading a book, but I sat up and watched. We watched, all of us watched, all the girls lounging lazily in the sun, stretched out across the lawn, all the girls sat up and watched, while the voice crooned across the garden.

I dreamed of a fly, a large, shiny fly, that I could see as though magnified, a monstrous fly, on the other side of my window, beating against the outside of my window. I could see the back of the fly, not its abdomen, which was a glossy gray green and glinted in the harsh light. The hard legs tapped against the glass loudly, as though they were made of metal of some sort. I could hear the fly tapping and buzzing loudly as though it were in my room, as though it were nearby, quite close to me, but I knew all the while it was outside. It beat and buzzed against the glass.

When I woke, suddenly, some time in the night, I realized it was not a fly but the branch of the pine tree outside my window, blown by the wind against the wooden shutters.

The three aunts addressed themselves to the potted shrimp, the three aunts with light bones and the same first initial to their names, as though the mother or the father or whoever had named them had gone in for alliteration for some rather absurd reason. I did not remember the initial, but my conjecture is that it was an M—M for Aunt Margery or Aunt Margaret or Aunt Maud or Aunt Milifred or Aunt May, even Aunt Millicent, some good name like that. The three maiden aunts with their dim lace collars and prim skirts and that Cassandra-like air, the three aunts who may very well have been maidens, who waved and clasped their hands in that anxious way and bent forward from the waist, leaned toward this girl, Daisy, in different shades of mauve.

The aunts said to this girl, shaking their heads, "You ought to change your dress," as though they knew in advance that their recommendation would only be ignored, as though they knew from experience that the matter was already out of their control, way out of their limited and feeble control, but knowing at the same time that they were still obliged to do their duty and say what they must say. They said, "You ought to change your dress," with a hopeless tone of voice, as though they had been saying things of this sort all of this girl's life and had never been listened to or heeded in any way.

Perhaps what the aunt or the aunts said was that she would not be warm enough, that she ought to take a woolie, that the weather might change, that rain had been predicted and she might catch cold, that she would catch her death, though that seems hardly likely, considering the heat of the day, or perhaps what they said had something to do with her dress, that there was something that was not quite suitable about the dress she was wearing that day, that the neckline was too low or the skirt was too short, or the fabric, which might have been silk, shantung or crepe de chine or something soft of that sort, was not appropriate, was too thin, too light, too transparent, was in some way reckless or not fitting for that day.

I do not know if the aunts were right about the dress, as I do not remember the dress, the color of the dress or the pattern or even the neckline or the hem, all I remember was the texture and the fact that, while the aunts were complaining about this girl's clothes or her lack of clothes, the girl had been whispering something to me through the delphinium.

She wanted to meet me down in the bamboo shoots at the bottom of the garden.

She had something for me, she said.

Miss B said something like, "I know we shouldn't, it'll be damp, we'll get rheumatism, but what a glorious night, what a lark!" with a giggle, the horse teeth protruding, on her back in a position that was probably described in the staff room as a position of abandon, even if it was abandon associated with the business of looking at the stars.

It was a clear night, all the stars visible, and Miss B was sharing, or attempting to share, her love of astronomy—the only constellation I remember was Orion, because of the belt and the sword; she must have dwelled on that, though I did not pay much attention to it. She sent forth a virtual fountain of information and fine spray into the air. It was noticed by someone that this Miss B, who lay in the grass, had her skirt well above her knees and—so it was said, but this was not true, this was in effect a gross calumny—had actually held the girl's hand.

Someone reported in the staff room that Miss B and a girl had been seen holding hands in the dark and lying together side by side, staring up at the stars. But in fact, even in her loneliness, even moved by the innumerable and unsurpassably bright stars, and perhaps by what she must have thought of as the desires of the flesh—something she undoubtedly tried to subdue, praying to God to still such turbulent and painful feelings, or moved by the whiteness of the girl's eyes or the paleness of the girl's skin, or something the girl might have said or not said—how would I know, after all, just what would move such a spinster to fall into such an abyss of silliness, Miss B had not quite dared to take the girl's hand, though her long upper lip had beaded with perspiration, and she had sighed very meaningfully.

I believe I can say in all fairness about that school that it was a place that had not yet bridged the gap from the time before the First World War to the time after the First World War, not to speak of the Second World War, not even to mention that. Inside that place, inside those thick, creeper-covered walls, we had perhaps heard murmurs of the Great War but had certainly never read about it, certainly never studied it in any way, so that when we emerged from that place, where we had been accustomed to see nothing but girls and girls and girls and English spinsters and the occasional cow, we emerged stunned, half-blind.

It was not something you could just forget. Or, in any case, it was not something I could forget. I was quite ill afterwards. I really mean it. I couldn't get myself out of bed. I tried not to think about it, but it kept coming back to me. I tried to get on with my work. I thought about the lives I'd saved. There was that little boy with bubble gum in his windpipe. Children should not be allowed to chew bubble gum. No one would give their kinders bubble gum if they could see what can happen, let me tell you.

You know, I tried to analyze what had happened. Sometimes I saw it as a symptom of something else, of some kind of violence endemic to that sort of society, of some lack of understanding between people in that place. Sometimes I even saw it as the key to the whole situation out there. Really, I did. At other times it just seemed to me something that could have happened anywhere, to anyone.

. . .

"I see," I suppose I said, "My, how late it is getting," or "Good heavens."

Such a terrible way to die.

I'm sure of it. At lunch that day at that place there was melba toast on the table. The thin blond slices curled on the edges, it seems to me, in the silver toast rack, as though burned by the heat. The light in the wine turned it to rose. There was a center bowl of flowers that stood among the blue and white china, perhaps of peonies, delphinium, and baby's breath, that drooped down, fanlike, onto the table. The loose blue petals of the delphinium had fallen onto the polished mahogany like shadows.

We must have drunk a little wine at lunch, already a glass or perhaps two. The aunts imbibed liberally and whispered, their pale cheeks flushing with the heat and the wine.

They spoke of this woman they called Lola. They spoke of the servants—the problem of the servants, how they no longer crossed to the other side of the street as they had done in the old days, when they saw you coming down the street, but now proceeded on their way, unconcerned. They spoke of other common subjects of conversation out there, as far as I remember, though I do not remember much about conversation out there.

It is quite as though I lived those sixteen years out there in silence. It was the sort of silence one finds in dreams.

I suppose I might have been sixteen, or perhaps seventeen, the day she died. Shortly afterward, I departed. Mother rushed me off to Austria, with the express purpose of procuring an English lord—she would have no other.

What I actually found in those mountains was snow. I saw snow there for the first time.

The tassels on the servant's band swung back and forth as he stretched across the table. The starch in the white uniform rustled. The servant tapped the bottle opener against the bottle of wine inquiringly.

Someone said, "My dear, do you think that dress is quite appropriate for lunch?"

I remember the glimmer of her face through the delphinium. Her face was quite white and even a little green around the arch of the nose, as she asked me to meet her at the bottom of the garden in the bamboo.

I suppose I recognized that glimmer of fear in her eyes even then. It was not the first time I had seen it. I suppose the green shade of the garden, the shimmer of the trees rising and falling in the air, seemed cooler to me than the house.

I remembered that glint of fear in Miss B's eyes.

There was a scandal at school I think I may have alluded to, a scandal that concerned a teacher, a Miss B. Not that there was anything that one could have remarked in any way that was in the least scandalous about this Miss B, the poor creature. On the contrary, as far as I remember, she was a rather plain, earnest, conscientious soul. She was one of those gray people who lead those ghastly gray lives, full of good intentions, remorse, and muddle, the inevitable muddle. I can see her peering through thick, misty glasses over my desk, one large, damp hand palm down on my book, admonishing me with great earnestness, the moisture spraying my face and the page of my book.

She was a young, big-boned teacher who had recently

come out from England and bored us all with her longing for the little lambs and the lilac, when the grass turned brown and the nights grew cold, in May. I suppose, thinking back over the business now, the roots of her scandal lay simply in her longing; it was simply her longing that led her astray.

It was longing, I suppose, that led Miss B to invite the girl into her room for biscuits and cocoa that night, having found the girl in the bathroom, out of bed and unable to sleep, already an insomniac and already coughing that dry cough at an early age. Instead of punishing the girl, who lay wrapped in a blanket in the bath—how many nights I had recourse to the bath and a book, while the rest of those girls breathed stertorously in their beds—this Miss B actually gave the girl biscuits and cocoa, when the girl obviously had no business with biscuits and cocoa, or Miss B's room, or particularly, Miss B's plaid rug and her hot water bottle. The girl was obviously supposed to be in her bed in the dormitory, sleeping, but was instead with Miss B on the end of her bed.

What finally brought about Miss B's fall, though, was not so much the biscuits and cocoa or even the constellations but, as I think I may have mentioned, the A on the maths test that was obtained quite easily, in a few minutes under the loquat trees.

The wind was tearing at the stunted pine outside my window. I wondered how those slender trees managed to remain planted in the thin, dry soil, how it was that they were not completely uprooted, dragged forth, and destroyed. But the roots held even in the wind that was driving the sand against the shutters. The branch was beating incessantly against the shutters. I grasped my inhaler and pumped, but to no avail. I was completely breathless, my throat ached, and I was certain I was feverish anew.

I wondered if the recovery from my illness had been incomplete. My long swim that morning having tired me out unduly, I would, I thought, be obliged to call a physician in, an Italian physician this time. Though I longed for slumber, I feared that in that sleep the effort required to breathe would be relinquished, and that I would perish. I propped up my pillows and lay with my eyes shut, laboring to draw breath.

She flirted with me. She was quite provocative at that dance. I told her people usually found doctors dull.

She said, That's not true at all, what could be more interesting than a handsome doctor. She laughed. She leaned towards me. She danced with her cheek against mine. Her cheek was cool and soft.

Surely you remember the dress she was wearing that day? I can still see the white of the dress and the white of her skin and the boat-shaped neckline.

How was I to have known that something like that would happen? How could anyone have suspected? Just the night before she was laughing, turning around on her heels, her dress opening up around her. I thought to myself, she's not like the rest.

What a man of his sort would actually be thinking was probably more on the lines of: this one will be easy game. Or: this one will be hot stuff.

. . .

As for Miss B, the spinster I believe I alluded to previously, she was never hot stuff, even under the dark leaves of the loquat trees.

I remember how the light pierced the leaves of the two loquat trees with sharp darts. The long branches with their dark thick leaves and succulent fruit swept down to the earth, enveloping the air and casting cool shadows on the sand. In the shadows of the trees the sand was smooth.

The A came forth quite easily with one or two meaningful pauses, the glimmer of a tear, an uplifted glance, and a light brush of the lips, with a *"Oh Miss B, you are quite wonderful"* breathed onto the powdered, pitted cheek, just a slight, skittery kiss in the dappled light of the loquat trees.

And all the while I watched the light in the leaves and the dark sand at our feet and vaguely the white-faced Miss B, as one watches a large and ungainly bird hop from a birdbath and ruffle its feathers in the sun.

The servants. Perhaps, after all, I thought, struggling for breath, this Summers girl had said something about a particular servant. I imagined it would have been something effusive, something hyperbolical, something on the sentimental side, such as, "He's a true gentleman," or "He's the only gentleman I know," or "He's one of nature's gentlemen," or even, "I really adore X." That might have been the sort of thing this Summers girl would have said about some servant or the other; X, whatever the man's name was, I could hardly have been expected to remember, I thought.

I had forgotten the kitchen. I had even forgotten the cool of the pantry and of the stone floor, the pantry with its large pull-out bins for flour and the scent of the oranges that were kept in large bags of hemp in a small recess that opened into darkness like a cave.

I remembered going along a narrow passageway and through a swing door to slip into the kitchen to steal the bottle of wine after lunch. I saw the narrow passageway with the Persian carpet and the Cries of London prints along the walls. I could see the servants clearly, standing chattering and laughing in the kitchen, rolling butter between wooden slats into small balls with serrated edges, several servants rolling butter between wooden slats into small balls to be placed on shell-shaped dishes on lettuce leaves.

I had forgotten the servant who was polishing, a tall man, though stooped. It is quite understandable to have forgotten the man. The man might have been polishing the floors, or polishing the silver, or polishing the shoes, or even polishing the soles of the shoes. He might have been polishing the floor, heaping up all the furniture into the center of the room and then getting down on his hands and knees and polishing the red tiles of the floor with small pads under his bare knees.

Or perhaps he had spread out old newspaper on the kitchen table and was polishing the silver, wearing away at the silver with those blunt, muffled movements, rubbing away incessantly at the monogram or any design on the silver until the monogram or the design became quite invisible.

One was inclined, quite naturally, in such a case, not to think of the servant, not to see the servant as a man, not to see the servant at all, but rather to think of him, to speak of him, as a polisher.

. . .

The wine was definitely red, a not unsatisfactory bottle of local wine, though perhaps a little heavy for the heat. In my opinion the wines of that place are often underestimated, particularly the red. The sherry is really rather special. I do advise you to try the sherry. It was, though, I suppose, hardly an appropriate digestive for two girls of sixteen. We drank, I believe, between the two of us, the whole bottle, this girl, this Summers girl being the one, if I remember correctly, who drank the greater part, down in the bamboo shoots.

Even had I remembered the incident, what happened that day in the bamboo shoots, it would not have been anything I ever mentioned to anyone, naturally. It was not the sort of thing one mentioned, as you'll understand. Actually, I'm not really certain the incident had any importance in my life.

What I remember were the closets and the clothes she wore, and for some reason, particularly, that essential garment, that soft and hard article, the foundation for all the rest of her elaborate toilet.

I remember the blue stars on the suspenders.

It was when it was removed completely and when she had filled her glass again that she came over to me in the evening, in the blue light, and reclined beside me, her white flesh spilling over me, engulfing me.

I asked myself afterward why I hadn't listened more carefully to what she was telling me. Why the hell didn't I listen? What a bloody fool. No one questioned me, thank God, even when I woke up shouting in my sleep.

Whoever did it got off scot-free, didn't he?

Why would anyone have wanted to do something like that to her, can you tell me? Hey, can you tell me?

They never found much of the body, or what they found was in bits and pieces. But, apparently, they could tell that in an attempt to save herself she had broken her wrists and her ankles. She had braced her legs and arms and broken her narrow bones even before it happened. Her wrists and ankles had snapped. Did you know that her narrow bones had broken as she tried to save herself?

It seemed to me then, as I lay there miserably, struggling for breath, pumping and twisting on my bed, that there was a dark-faced man in the dream, but I was not certain of that.

I rose from my bed and in an effort to breathe opened the windows and the shutters on the midnight sky. I could hear the sound of the waves, whipped by the wind, and see the white shadows spread along the shore. The darkness seemed to move gradually, covering all of the land, which appeared, then, like some shipwreck, to be gradually sinking into the sea. The town huddled precariously on the edge of complete obscurity. Only a few lights still glistened on the water. There were no sounds but that of the recurring waves of wind and the fainter one of the waves on the shore.

All I knew was that the wind was blowing ceaselessly and that this Summers girl had been telling me of someone in a dream.

I wondered if it would be wise to call a physician, an Italian physician this time. If I was obliged to call the physician, I knew what he would prescribe: cortisone, more cortisone. I was afraid of the moon face. A pale moon face.

I am careful with my white skin.

. . .

The bottle of wine we stole from the cool of the pantry was definitely red.

I remembered the man, the servant this Summers girl may have mentioned. I saw him sitting at the wooden table in the pantry. I noticed the pink palms of his black hands. He was polishing with blunt, incessant gestures, his khaki uniform rustling. Perhaps that was the man of whom this Summers girl said something hyperbolical, some sort of jejune statement, that he was one of nature's gentlemen, or perhaps even that she adored him. A thin, tall man, probably a Zulu, a man so thin he looked as though he had run out of things to polish and had started on himself.

I think, actually, all things considered, that what the man was polishing were the soles of the shoes. He had spread newspaper out across the table, and—I'm quite certain of this now; I can see the high shine on the bottom of the shoes and hear the sound of the crinkling of the newspaper and the cloth rubbing against the shoe—he was polishing the soles of the brown lace-up shoes, the heavy brown lace-up shoes we were obliged to wear for school.

He looked up at this Summers girl, as we came into the room to steal a bottle of wine, and lifted his head and smiled at us in an amused way, as though there was something rather delightful and at the same time a great source of merriment in this girl's presence. He said, "Cluck, Cluck, Dizzy," clicking his tongue against his palate and saying a name which, I presumed, was the name he used for her, a name he had given her as the Zulus are wont to do, making up some name for this girl. "Cluck, Cluck, Dizzy," he said and laughed, and she laughed, too, I seem to remember, as though the two of them shared some intimate secret, though I could not imagine, naturally, what sort of secret they might have shared. Perhaps that was the man this girl said she adored in that effusive way, and that was the extent of their conversation.

I remember the servant's name. The man was called Justice.

She caught our gaze, as one grasps a shell in the palm of a hand. A girl, perhaps it was this Summers girl, with light hair and a certain light in the skin, who ran barefooted, with her tunic tucked up in her knickers—all of which was, of course, not permitted: the running and the bare feet and the tunic tucked up into the knickers—across the grass to the fish pond.

She took a great, long, ridiculous leap, tucking her legs up in the air and opening her arms and her mouth wide, as though she were opening herself up to the flowers or the garden or the girls watching or perhaps even one particular girl watching, making that ridiculous, rash leap from the stone arch across the fish pond, so that she rose up into the air, all light, like an air ball, and then fell with a crash into the fish pond, so that we were sure, or I was certainly sure, that the girl would shatter completely, would splinter like glass, break her thin arms and legs, break every light bone in her body—there was not much to the girl, you know, hardly even a girl, as I remember, rather more of a child; and the pond was not deep, after all, could hardly have been more than a couple of feet deep—and came up with her green tunic and her white, short-sleeved shirt, transparent and clinging to the new curves of her body and a lily pad between her teeth and laughed, actually laughed with what I am obliged to call crazy abandon.

A quite ridiculous, rather hysterical thing to do. Still, the sort of thing only someone who felt she could do anything and get away with it would do. I was aware, of course, that it was a rather frightening thing to do, a dangerous thing, but one, I suppose, that broke the monotony of the day.

Perhaps what I fear more than anything else is ennui. It is that which really kills, is it not?

There was a wind blowing mournfully, that day in the bamboo shoots at this girl's place, like the wind that continued to blow as I lay propped up on white pillows, disturbing the quiescence of the night and interrupting my thoughts.

Despite the wind it was hot even in the bamboo shoots.

This girl the man called Daisy took me down into the bamboo shoots at the bottom of the garden after lunch. I am not certain why we descended into the bamboo shoots, except that that part of the garden appeared to be cooler and lay at a certain distance from the house.

There was a small stream down there and a stile—she may have said something about the stile being a wishing stile, about wanting to wish some wish, and that each time one crossed the stile one could wish a wish that would come true. At any rate it was a stile that crossed over the stream, and the sound of the running water seemed to cool the air. What I was thinking of, I suppose, was the sound of the water running over the stones and the low wind stirring the long grass.

Actually, I am not certain whose suggestion it was to go down into that part of the garden. Perhaps I was mistaken about what the girl was whispering to me through the delphinium, though I was not mistaken about the fear in her face. The suggestion may even have been my own. It is even possible that the wine and the cigarettes were my idea. It was certainly not something I had ever done before. I had certainly not gone down there to smoke cigarettes and drink wine before.

It seems to me we sat in a haze of smoke. We sat there smoking one cigarette after the other, mechanically. I am almost certain that I smoked eight of them, though the figure may be completely apocryphal. It was not my habit to smoke cigarettes or to drink anything other than milk. I do not believe I had ever smoked a cigarette before except for those nauseous puffs to light Mother's cigarettes in the car on the lengthy car trips taken across the highveld. That day this girl carried in the pocket of her skirt a box of cigarettes and slipped under her arm a stolen bottle of wine. I do not remember much about the girl, or why we were smoking cigarettes, or why we were going down into the bamboo shoots, but I can see the box of cigarettes quite clearly. I remember the box with the yellow camel wrapped in cellophane paper and how the box glinted in the bright light.

Whether this girl led me or I led her down into the bamboo shoots, I do not remember. It was obviously of no importance.

The place I can see quite clearly.

It was a treeless stretch of flat land where the veld ran wild and the bamboo grew thick. In the long grass, burrs were everywhere and caught in socks or stockings. I suppose it must have been around two or three in the afternoon, when this girl took me down, or I took her down, into the bamboo to smoke cigarettes, the light so bright that the flame of the matches we used was invisible, the heat so wearying that the effort of walking across the pink-gray haze of the veld down into the bamboo shoots, the continued effort of being at least polite, was almost too great. I followed, or I led, this girl down into the bamboo, because to stay in the trapped heat of the house or to face the heat of the garden came to much the same thing, and I knew, I suppose, even then, as one knows things of that sort, that we were going down into the bamboo not only to smoke cigarettes but to do something else that this girl had in mind.

She lifted up the covers on the hollow darkness of the bed and covered us over. It was stiflingly hot under the linen sheet, under the mohair blanket and the pink silk eiderdown. She pulled the eiderdown over our heads and dragged me down into the sheets, so that the light flickered through feebly, and the air was trapped.

To me it smelled down there of buried objects, a dark, mysterious smell.

Her flesh fell in damp white folds, covering me.

I suppose she knew then that something would occur that night. I suppose this girl, this Summers girl, might have known all that day that something would happen to her. Perhaps, in some strange way that was actually what she wanted. Or it may have been when we crossed the stile that led from the smooth green lawns to the long grass of the wild veld that she knew what would happen. Not that I troubled myself with what the girl was thinking; I was not thinking about the girl at all, as far as I remember. I was listening to the cooling sound of the water, running over the stones, and the moaning of the wind in the bamboo. I was watching the low wind in the long grass, and for all I know, what actually happened may have come upon her like a sudden storm, without warning.

Perhaps I remember some of this more clearly than you do because I kept a diary during that period of my life. I wrote down some of my feelings and thoughts after she died. It helped me to write about it. I remember how, after the dance, I wanted to take her out somewhere. I wanted to be on my own with her.

I wanted to hold her in my arms, to own her. She had something about her, something I couldn't quite put my finger on, as though it was enough just to stand there and be who she was: Daisy Summers.

It has never been enough to be who I am.

Whatever he may have written in his diary, if he actually kept one, which seems to me rather doubtful or anyway quite absurd—just imagine all those people sitting there, scribbling down their thoughts and feelings madly, probably thinking someone might read them some day, as though anyone could care—what he probably wanted was to own her and the house and the jacaranda trees and the lawns that stretched out like a hand to the hills. What he wanted was to own the house and the land and the veld and even the bamboo shoots.

Naturally, I do not remember exactly what the man said. The man's words had little interest for me.

I said, "I wonder what it's like to be dead," or made some such fatuous remark in reference to the hallowed but still rotting bones of the High Commissioner, which lay beneath me.

I do not remember exactly what the girl replied—I suppose it might have been this Summers girl—though I believe she mumbled some sort of rash, romantic statement about love, the sort of thing one says at fourteen or fifteen, something about a "pleasure unto death," as she lay on the High Commissioner's grave—obviously something she must have read somewhere.

We took off our shirts and lay side by side with our new breasts to the sky, reciting Keats or perhaps Wordsworth—if I remember rightly we used to compete to see who could remember the most, reciting as fast as we could, running through the lines breathlessly, until someone came to a stop: "the little lines of sportive wood run wild" or some such lines, feeling the cool of the marble on the backs of our bare legs and the breeze on our damp skin, listening to the sound of the cicadas shrilling. We rose and drank from the acrid water of the small stream that ran down the side of the *koppie* and splashed the water on our faces.

It was there, I believe, that I first felt desire.

I do not remember the sequence of events down in the bamboo shoots. Why should I have remembered something like that? Mostly I remember that heavy, humid heat that settled down over us despite the wind, suffocatingly, like a steel trap, and the languorous sound of the waves, as they slapped lazily onto the shore and the moan of the hot breeze in the bamboo.

I remember how my head ached from the wine and the heat and the smoke. I do know that this Summers girl was sucking on the bottle of wine and puffing on the cigarettes and tilting the wine bottle back so that the liquid rushed into her mouth, her lips slack. Then she wiped the top of the bottle carelessly with the palm of her hand and handed it over to me, leaning toward me.

Somehow her presence seemed to cause the heat to increase immoderately.

She was flushed, hot-eyed, and her touch was clammy.

When the dark, bitter liquid oozed onto my palate, I was filled with nausea.

The truth is there is not much kindness in human nature, not much love or charity.

The light in the dormitory was silver. A moon as perfectly round as a child's yellow sticker, pasted on a transparent blue, tissue-paper sky, lit up the room. The air was scented with the skin of an orange and the eucalyptus that grew by the window. The girl sat in the windowsill in the silence of the sleeping dormitory.

The game was over and the girl, I suppose it might have been this Summers girl, was left naked, apart from her fluffy pink slippers. She leaned indolently against the window frame, her legs curled before her. The light of the moon illuminated her face; her skin was lit as the sky above her but with a light that seemed to come, unlike the moon's, from within: wide-spaced eyes, moist lips parted, silver.

She leaned forward toward me with a soft, wilting movement that was almost mournful. My eye was drawn to her wrist, to the pale skin of her wrist, as she made a gesture of invitation; this girl was asking me to come to her side in the window seat.

"I'm jealous of you," she said.

"Jealous, why jealous? You're in the swimming team

and the hockey team and the tennis team, and I'm not," I said.

"Not jealous like that. I want you to be my friend," she said fiercely.

"I am your friend. Of course, I'm your friend," I said.

"But only my friend, not anyone else's friend," she said.

Outside the window the night watchman tramped, his feet in heavy, lace-up shoes, crunching the gravel of the pathway, the beam of his torch flickering in the soft yellow of the mimosa and the slender, sickle-shaped leaves of the eucalyptus trees.

"You want to come in my bed?" this girl, this Daisy—I suppose it was—said and kicked off her slippers and jumped down into the rumpled sheets of her bed. "Oh, come on," she said and stretched out her hand to me.

She had a loose, lithe wrist that held my gaze.

I can see the flowers of that garden: the faded, pink-and-white sweet peas as fragile and translucent as a girl's skin, the delicate blue delphinium—was it? like the shadows around the eyes and the hollows of the hips, the stiff, proud strelitzias, the arms reaching out with cupidity, the bell-shaped columbine in the shade, the puerile sex, and the hollyhocks, the striding legs.

I can hear the sound of the surf breaking on the beach below, that warm, shark-infested water, those brown, churning waters that broke along the edge of the shore.

Naturally, I do not remember how she went from puffing on a cigarette and sipping wine from the bottle—what was that bottle of wine, perhaps a bottle of Boschendaal?—

wiping off the neck of the bottle with the palm of her hand and passing it to me, to touching me in the bamboo shoots.

I remember the haze and the heat that made my dress adhere to my skin, my temples grow damp, my hair cling to the nape of my neck, and the perspiration mist my view so that through the smoke of the cigarettes this girl's form came to me as a light, moving blur.

Perhaps a little of the wine had spilled from the side of my mouth, was actually running down my chin, and she wiped my chin and let her hand linger on my face and then on my chest, or I spilled some wine on the bodice of my dress, and she moistened her handkerchief and sponged my chest with increasing tenderness, or she burst into tears and leaned her head against my breast longingly, or she just touched my hand or just touched me with her hot gaze.

I only know that this assault upon my body and the liquor filled me with nausea.

The man made a little bow to us, just leaned forward slightly from the waist, a rather grave, awkward gesture, I seem to remember, that acknowledged our presence. At the same time, there was something rather eager about the way the man in the shiny suit bowed toward us as he stood waiting on the *stoep*. I glanced at the young man in the shiny, ill-fitting suit and then back at this girl, this Summers girl, but it seems to me that she was hardly aware of the man. She was looking at me, and she was laughing, her laughter loud, childlike, bright, and as brittle as cut-glass. Then I suppose she waved to the man or made some gesture acknowledging the presence of the man, who leaned forward slightly with that grave, stiff gesture, bowing toward us as he stood on the *stoep*.

. . .

Of course, I realized she had been drinking. I could tell she'd had a hell of a lot to drink.

"Oh, everyone drinks out there," I suppose I said with indifference.

He may have tried to tell me something like that. Perhaps the man I met on the terrace told me this Summers girl had seemed excited that afternoon at tea or at coffee, that we had come up out of the bamboo, and she had seemed excited in some way. Perhaps those were the sort of words he would have used, but whatever the words were, it seems to me that that was what the man had implied.

Whatever he said, what he probably thought was, this one will be hot stuff.

She was very pale.

She seemed anxious, or she was excited.

Anyway, she was distracted. The night before she had flirted, but that afternoon she couldn't sit still at tea. She crumbled a scone with the tips of her fingers. She stood at the window and watched the garden. Her look wasn't at me anymore, a non-gaze; her attention span was short. She was twisting her pearls around her fingers. She got up and sat down.

She looked as transparent as the glass behind her.

I suppose the man I met in Gerzett, or had met many years before Gerzett, kept telling me how restless this Summers girl seemed, how she stood at the window, watching for someone.

. . .

You both came up from the bottom of the garden, from the bamboo shoots. She wasn't looking at me. She was humming something under her breath, maybe, or singing some song or laughing or just staring.

It was enough to drive a fellow mad, it was enough to drive you crazy.

Perhaps he said something of that sort.

She wandered out into the garden. She seemed drawn out into the garden. She looked as though she was floating across the gravel in that white dress and high-heeled sandals. She went down the driveway toward the white gate, as though she were already a ghost.

I followed her.

What he was undoubtedly thinking was that he wanted to do to her, was determined to do to her, what he eventually did that night with me in the mountains. Or, I thought, that might have been what the man had been telling me that night after he had made love to me, but I could not be quite sure. I really had not been listening to the man, even then. Quite honestly nothing much he had said had registered at the time, and afterward I was not sure at all if that was what the man in Gerzett had said.

My body was burning. My head ached quite intolerably. I had the impression that appalling night would never end. Hours and hours of time seemed to have passed without day becoming any closer. Sleep eluded me completely. Like quicksilver, the more I attempted to grasp it, the more it slipped from me. There were moments when it seemed imminent, but then it escaped me, like a dream one attempts to remember, or a name. Each time I rose up on one elbow to look at my traveling clock on the bedside table, the green illuminated hands of the clock seemed hardly to have moved. I would have suspected the clock had stopped except for the sound of the regular, loud ticking.

Beside the sound of the clock's ticking I kept hearing, every now and then, particularly when there was a lull in the sighing of the wind, the sound of the shiver of glass, as though great numbers of crystal bowls were breaking on stone floors in innumerable empty rooms; over and over again I heard the echo of the shiver of glass. It was this sound, the sound of crystal breaking, that was making my head ache quite intolerably.

In the half dark of my room the outside world seemed quite distant. I could not hear the sound of a human voice. All I could hear then was the sighing of the wind and the sea. That room seemed suddenly unfamiliar to me. Even the precious objects of my room, my books on the bedside table, the silver brush and comb set, the photo of Mother in its silver frame, the bottles and jars on the dressing table, the petit-point cushion I had worked myself, the straw bag slung over the arm of a chair, all of these things that were so familiar to me, seemed not only to have no importance at all but to be almost unknown.

I switched off the bedside lamp then and lay in complete darkness. Though I could see almost nothing I was immediately certain of a presence in the dark of the room as though this figure had waited for complete obscurity to come to me; someone, I sensed, was sitting motionless and as if fascinated, staring at me from the stool before the dressing table.

For a moment—I felt quite ill as I made it out—I took

this shape to be that of the man I had met on the terrace in Gerzett. I lay there quite helplessly, unable to move. The sight of what I took to be the man on the terrace had something inexplicably sinister about it. It appeared to be a dangerous living presence, the presence of an enemy, or even of a criminal. I was too terrified to call out.

Then the man appeared to move slightly, turning the head and to my increasing horror I realized that the figure was not that of a man at all but of a young woman. The woman laid down whatever it was she held in her hands and seemed to rise slowly, her whole form elongated like a monstrous shadow on a wall, bending over me.

I kept my eyes averted and watched, with all the energy I could muster, the faint beam of lighter darkness that penetrated the shutters. I had the impression that if I could just keep staring at that faint beam of something that was not even light but rather something less than the dark, I would be safe.

The dark shadow of a woman cried out, "Listen to me, please listen to me."

The shadow seemed to bend nearer, reaching out to me, grasping at my body, clinging to me, touching my face and neck. The fingers seemed to reach for my throat.

"Let me go!" I screamed.

"Dearheart!"

I reached out and pushed the shadow from me, the scream repeating itself in my brain.

In order to rid myself of the terrible, hovering form, I shut my eyes and found myself immediately walking under an alley of jacarandas. The jacarandas were lit up with Chinese lanterns that hung from the branches. I could hear the faint squelch of the mauve blossoms under my bare feet. The ground was damp and the ooze of the flowers as slippery as blood.

All the time it was happening I could hear the rain; it was raining hard. I could hear the rain coming down and the wind whipping up the waves that broke on the sand, wearing away at the dunes.

I remembered walking along a narrow path on the edge of the cliff. The jagged outline of parts of that coast has an almost spectral look. A steep, craggy, treeless surface drops precipitously to the turbid sea below, worn away by the great waves constantly breaking over the years. It is an isolated place, one that attracted only the most hardy of the settlers of that land. Heat, humidity, dense bush, fever, native raiding kept all but the tenacious away. Only an occasional house, half covered with thick vegetation, perches precariously on the side of the cliff.

There was no one in sight that afternoon, as I recall. There was no sound but that of the waves and the wind beating in the strelitzia leaves. In the distance, below me, I could see the white sand of the beach. The glare drowned all of this in a gray haze.

I walked barefoot along the path, nauseous and dizzy from the wine, the cigarettes, or perhaps from the prominence of the cliff. My head ached intolerably. I must have removed my sandals, carried them in one hand. I suppose I felt the need of some sea air or a little exercise, or perhaps I simply wished to be alone. I toiled somewhat breathlessly along the path, leaning forward, my toes splayed in sand and grass.

I came upon the wreck of an automobile that had, I suppose, been driven down the narrow path to the edge of the cliff and left there to wallow in mud, half covered with creepers and long grass, turned on its side with two wheels in the air. One wheel was missing. The rotting thing looked as dead as the carcass of some wild animal. Behind the wreck the ragged leaves of the strelitzia trees hung over the rock and sand, beating in the wind.

I realized I was mistaken about the sleeves, actually, not mistaken about the sleeves so much as mistaken about where this Summers girl was standing when her sleeves were fluttering. It was not in the large room with the bay window but rather, on the cliff by the sea. It was not morning but twilight.

Twilight had seemed to come early, as the sky was darkened by clouds. Thunder rumbled in the distance. The light was dim on the cliff though the sky was still a pale blue in patches, and the wind that blew in dusty gusts whipped the clouds fast across the sky.

It was the putting on and the taking off of the clothes that I used to watch.

It was on the cliff that her damp sleeves fluttered around her honey-hued arms and below the dark waves surged forward, wearing away at sand and rock.

In her high heels and her white dress and the evening light she seemed to float across the gravel. She already looked like a ghost. It was the last thing anyone saw of her. She walked down the stone steps and across the grass.

I swear that was the last thing I saw of her.

. . .

She seemed excited, flushed and excited.

I am not certain of what the man on the terrace said, but what I do know is that it rained the night this Summers girl died. I remember the rain. It was the same sort of white rain we had at Mother's funeral. I do not remember what day of the week it was or even which month, but I remember the white rain, a short sudden downpour and then a pause filled with the rumbling of thunder and flashes of lightning and then the white rain that turned to hail and came accompanied by forked lightning alternating with sheet lightning, illuminating the sky.

Even when it began to rain, the heavy drops spattering the earth, I suppose she had not turned to go inside but had gone on walking, in the shadows of the strelitzia trees, on the narrow path at the edge of the cliff, in the half dark, the rain streaming down her face, the rain in her hair, and her dress clinging to her body.

As a matter of fact, you know, quite sincerely, I have always enjoyed those tropical storms—the drama of it all—the unleashing of nature's wild forces. Such storms arouse in me a rather strange excitement, a vague and pleasant warmth that I hesitate to define. I can only say I like to see the sky suddenly lit up, entirely blanched for a second with a roll and a crack, or a great line of white fire scrawled across the gray heavens.

As children, when there was a storm we were always told to come in out of the water if we were swimming and not to huddle under a tree, that the forked lightning might strike us dead, or the heavy trunk of a tree might fall upon us and crush us.

The hail was sometimes as big as rocks out there, coming down and cutting up awnings, shredding the leaves of the trees and crushing the petals of flowers.

Perhaps the man in Gerzett had tried to tell me about this place, which he had visited as a young man.

The bathing near there is dangerous. In fact, despite the white beaches it is impossible to bathe down there except in small, restricted areas where shark nets are set up, and a lifesaver runs rather frantically back and forth blowing his yellow whistle with alarm if any of the bathers should stray outside the nets.

Not only are there sharks, but the backwash is strong and rip tides not uncommon. The waves rise slowly to great heights and bear down with a crash, and if one is caught in their passionate grip, they hold one down and roll one over repeatedly, grinding one against the sand until one almost suffocates before being thrown up onto the beach as limp as a piece of seaweed.

Mostly, the bathers, driven into the brown waters by the extreme heat, huddle together, remaining on the edge, jumping up and down, screaming, bumping into one another, pushing playfully, and occasionally ducking a little desperately under the huge waves.

Sometimes a shark makes its way through the nets and remains trapped amongst the bathers. There were several shark attacks written up in the papers; one man lost a leg just wading knee deep in the brown turbid waters.

I could see the flowers of the garden, the soft pink-and-white sweet peas that clustered in drooping bushes along the tennis court, the shadowy blue delphinium, the petals falling around the stems. It was that moment of the year when the spring flowers are almost over, and summer's blooms have yet to begin.

Constantly, in the distance, there was the sound of the vast waves dashing against sand and rock, wearing away at the cliff, that shelved down steeply into the sea.

As for this Summers girl's, this Daisy's, exact words, I remembered only a sentence or two, when I had remembered everything, or as much as I will ever remember, I believe.

I was under the impression, then, that she had begun the conversation we had that day with something that had occurred at school, perhaps something about the fish pond, or one of the teachers, or even the grave, the High Commissioner's grave.

When I came back that night the rain had ceased, though like the wind on the island it was to start up again.

Her dress was soaked and clinging to her body, and her hair was dripping.

She told me she was going for a walk to get some air. She had to go alone. I followed her for a way.

Far out on the horizon a ship made a difficult passage, tossed about wildly in the rain and the mist. From the sandy path where I walked along the edge of the cliff I could just make out the blurred shape of a ship.

When the rain began to fall, I could just have continued and found my way back to the house by another of the paths that led back to the house, a path that would probably have been shorter than turning back on the way I had already covered. But the rain was in my eyes, and my head was still throbbing from the heat and from the wine and the cigarettes. I suppose I could not face the effort needed to take another path.

It did not seem very important which path I took.

Besides, I was not quite sure of any other way. The rough paths through the bush had been cut by a native with a *panga*. Some of the paths had become almost impassable where the bush had pushed through and grown back.

Did I mention, I have always been afraid of snakes? The bush there is full of green and black mambas, which hang unseen from the branches. I could feel the live snakes out there, twisted around thick branches in the half dark of the twilight and the rain.

It seemed more prudent to turn back and face the dangers I already knew.

She stood there with her damp dress clinging to her body and her knees bare and her damp hair close to her head and the wet sleeves flapping in the wind.

As I leaned forward with my bare toes in the sand, I realized the dogs had come after me when I left the house; I suppose they had pushed open the screen kitchen door and followed me; the dogs bounded around me joyfully.

There were two fluffy gray-white dogs, Airedales, it seems to me, who ran on ahead at times and ran back to me, to make sure I was following, or just circled my feet, jumping up to catch at my hands, pawing the front of my dress excitedly. They stopped to sniff around that wrecked car, almost as though it possessed some particular attraction, barking at the thing excitedly, as though it were an animal of some sort. The dogs made little excited sallies into the bush, sniffing at mysterious scents, crashing back through the bush to come to me, or chasing unseen small animals or possibly even a snake. From time to time I caught sight of an ear or the top of a head in the thick underbrush.

Two gray-white, curly-haired dogs, probably Airedales, were barking at my feet clamorously.

Perhaps the dogs had raced on ahead at that point, and I had followed them, thinking it would be safer to remain with the dogs, though, probably, another path would have been shorter and might even, for all I know, have been wider. It did not seem to make much difference with the rain falling and the lightning flashing.

At first I probably thought it was a rock, a faint white glimmer of something on the side of the cliff. I could see with difficulty. As I walked toward the house across the sand path, on the edge of the cliff, the rain was in my face, thrown against me, beating against me, driving me back. The wind blew the rain and my unpinned hair into my face. I pulled the hood of my jacket over my head and leaned forward into the wind. I toiled steadily onward with something quite like determination, going toward what, in the murky light, I took for a rock.

I was thinking, I suppose, if I was thinking of anything at all, of the throbbing of my head and of removing my wet clothes, which already clung to me, and of drying my damp hair, and I may have been thinking of Mother, who had promised to come and fetch me after tea.

I'm sure she was waiting for you.

Why the hell did you just go off, without even drinking any tea? Don't you remember anything about that after-

noon? I could have sworn it was you. You flicked your hair behind your head just like that, with your nails flashing, and walked out, without saying anything at all. I can remember those nails, the length of them, that pearly, pink-white sheen and the slightly blue tips. You just walked down the path, going toward the sea. You never looked back. Surely you must remember this girl?

I do not ask much of people, I said.

At that moment I only asked to be left alone—anything to be left alone.

Her eyes filling with pleasure, Mother slowly liberated her full white form from the constriction of all her garments and from the dark hair that hung down, curtainingly. She sighed softly and came over to me to offer a pleasure I had long since ceased to enjoy.

The bed was falling beneath me.

Of course, I no longer remember exactly what the man told me, nor do I know whether he told me the truth. There were things he said which I doubted, certain information I took with a pinch of salt. I can only tell you what I think I remember he said, and what I think happened that night.

When I came back, the rain had ceased, though like the wind on the island it was to start up again. Mother was waiting in her automobile. It was not really worth saying good-bye. Besides, the aunts were probably still resting.

When I came closer, I realized it was not a rock.

I was mainly conscious of that white rain. I felt as

though a white curtain had come down between me and the world beyond.

I would have done anything to be rid of clinging hands, tears, the strain of being polite, to retrieve the silence, to remove the wet, clinging clothes, to dry my hair.

Her dress was soaked and clinging to her body, and her hair was dripping.

I'm certain I saw you on that day at that place. I could swear it was at a luncheon or a dinner or perhaps it was tea. Was that it?

We had tea in the lounge. Daisy was standing by the window, by the heavy curtains, in that white dress. You refused the tea. I remember the way you refused the tea.

I remember the eyes, the whiteness of the eyes, and the long nails, the way you swept your hair back from your face with the flick of your nails. I remember the way you looked out the window, as though you couldn't have cared less.

You were not listening to what anyone said.

This is one possible way it might have happened.

"Oh, listen to me, please, just this once, can't you listen to me just this once?" she said, leaning toward me, clasping her arms around my neck, pressing her wet cheek to mine.

I was conscious mainly of the sound of the rain falling and less distinctly of the sea beneath us heaving.

It was not that I was unable to see her in that light. In the flashes of lightning I could actually see her quite clearly. I could see how her sleeves flapped in the wind, those loose sleeves of that light, almost transparent stuff. I knew she was crying; I noted it distinctly, but as though it were coming from a great distance. Even in that flickering light I could see the wet, slack mouth, the wide lips, the red eyes, the tears, hear the sobs, but the sound of this crying touched me as little as the sound of the sea. I felt nothing; only each time she sobbed, the pressure of her arms around my neck grew greater.

The rain fell as though someone were throwing it at me directly.

The truth is that there is almost nothing as tiresome as unwanted love.

The night was steamy, the earth sodden, and the smell of rain bitter. She slumped forward into the dark with great weariness; it was as though her body were suddenly heavy, as though all her limbs had acquired a great weight.

I had not really noticed how much wine she had drunk. She was murmuring things to me, and her face was damp with the rain or with tears.

I rose from my damp bed, breathless, the perspiration running across my temples. I thought of calling the physician then, gasping as I was for breath. The Italian physician, like the Swiss one, might tell me more lies, might wrap up his prescription with a string of elegant compliments, but in the end he would only prescribe more cortisone, I knew that. It was obvious to me then that cortisone was not the cure for what ailed me. There was no cure for it.

She stood between the tubs of hydrangeas, under the light on the stoep, and told me to go. She said she was going for a walk.

I was under the impression she was going to find you. I followed her a little way.

He must have told me that or something like that.

I do know that there was no moon that night. Even when the rain had stopped, there was no moon and no stars, only the thick, steamy dark, the pounding of the surf, and the smell of bitter earth.

Perhaps it happened this way. Though the rain was in my eyes, and my head throbbed from the heat and the wine, I could see it all distinctly, but from a great distance, and through, as it were, someone else's eyes. The rain continued to pelt down about us. The sound of the waves grew wilder. The light had turned a yellowish gray. Flashes of lightning knifed across the sky almost continuously. Far out on the horizon I caught glimpses of a ship tossed about without mercy.

Something was clinging, pulling at my neck, dragging me down. Something white and heavy was clinging to me. I could smell the familiar acrid breath and feel the damp, clammy hands. I needed space, I needed to breathe. Naturally, I tried to fling it from me. Half consciously, quite mechanically, I thrust it from me.

Suddenly, it was as if I was filled with a great strength that was not my own. I was filled with a new sense of power. I heaved the weight backward from me. I heaved the weight into what seemed a not imperfect place for something of that kind.

Then, as though it was I who had lost my footing in the sand, the earth began to tilt and heave, the lightning cracked the sky. For a moment I felt as though I had been struck. A great sheet of whiteness blinded me. I was conscious only of the cracking of the thunder and the sound of the sea. But as soon as the thing was done, I reclaimed my own strength. I felt a warmth run through me, a certain heat spread through my body. I was perspiring and weak. I wished only to sleep.

She cried out, but weakly.

They found parts of the body the next morning in the sand. In an attempt to slow her fall, she had broken her wrists.

I do remember the color of her eyes now; they were blue, actually, the lashes long and dark. I remember the color of the hair, a dark blond, and the shape of the face, the forehead broad and the chin small and pointed. It was an ordinary face, not a strong face or a particularly distinguished face, apart from the coloring, the flush that rose from the neck into the cheeks.

I rose and stood at the window. I thought of this Summers girl who was dead.

I no longer remember how they informed me of her death. Perhaps one of the aunts telephoned me, or I may have read an account in the paper. What I thought of then was this Summers girl, as she fell down into the sea. I saw her face, as she lifted her head toward me, her mouth open, her hair plastered to her temples. I could see in her eyes the astonishment at this ultimate outrage. I noticed her body, lit up by the flash of lightning, as she slithered across the wet rock, her fingers scrabbling furiously for some hold on sand or stone, clinging to the smallest tuft of grass or moss, stretching her legs and arms out, her limbs rigid in an attempt to slow her fall. Finally, though, she dropped into the void of the sea. I could see her, as she lay on the surface of the water, face down, the sleeves of her white dress filled with air, puffed up, rather like those plastic wings children wear to learn to swim.

Clouds suddenly gathered in a sullen, overhanging sky, and the gulls swooped down low over the sea, the blue of the water reflected in the white breasts of the birds. It had not grown cooler. The temperature had not dropped, then, as it had on the island during the night I had lain awake, recollecting.

Once I had remembered what had happened, or what I thought had happened, I felt quite calm again. I breathed more easily. My head no longer ached. The peace of the early morning rippled over me like a light wave.

In the end what difference did it make that this one life had been lost, that this young girl had died, while I had gone on living?

Surely, it made not the least difference.

Obviously, now, I would never again be bothered by the creaking of the crepe-soled shoes of the man I thought I had met in Gerzett.

I opened the shutters on the faint light.

It was hardly morning. The moon had waned, but the sun had not yet risen, and the sea still merged with the sky. Gradually, the faintest flush of pale light brushed the waters and the heavens. Pink, orange, and red bands spread like the fingers of a hand, reaching across the sky. The sea was flat and calm. As the sun rose higher, the whitewashed houses, like some stark stage set perched on the side of the rocky coast, glimmered faintly, gradually emerging from the night. The island stretched before me, a barren place of stunted tree and evanescently flowering bush, caught in the midst of the winds from the north and the south, hardly changed by years of invasion, ransack, and pillage, by violence and death. The invaders had come and gone and left precious little behind but their dreams.

I stood there watching the sea that surrounded it all. Only the smallest pale wave lifted itself, almost imperceptibly, and spilled its foam-flecked translucence onto the beach, with so soft a murmur as to be almost inaudible. One after the other the waves rose and fell, each drawing a thin line on the white sand before the next wave smoothed away even that faint trace. The waves rose and fell, rose and fell, gently. The wind, I was sure, had died.

A NOTE ON THE TYPE

The text of this book was set in Electra, a type face designed by W(illiam) A(ddison) Dwiggins (1880–1956) for the Mergenthaler Linotype Company and first made available in 1935. Electra cannot be classified as either "modern" or "old style." It is not based on any historical model, and hence does not echo any particular period or style of type design. It avoids the extreme contrast between thick and thin elements that marks most modern faces, and it is without eccentricities that catch the eye and interfere with reading. In general, Electra is a simple, readable type face that attempts to give a feeling of fluidity, power, and speed.

W. A. Dwiggins began an association with the Mergenthaler Linotype Company in 1929 and over the next 27 years designed a number of book types, including Metro, Electra, Caledonia, Eldorado, and Falcon.

Composed by PennSet, Inc., Bloomsburg, Pennsylvania. Printed and bound by The Haddon Craftsmen, Inc., Scranton, Pennsylvania. Designed by Julie Duquet.